Mischief and Mayhem in Mistletoe

Mistletoe Treasures
Book 1

By

Ronna M. Bacon

Dedicated to my niece, Fiona, who loves Christmas stories and asked if I had written one. This one is for you, Fiona. Luv you lots.

Verses

Jeremiah 29:13. You will seek me and find me when you seek me with all your heart.

I Chronicles 16:11. Look to the Lord and his strength; seek his face always.

New King James Version

Table of Contents

He stood over the grave, tears flowing down his face, not wanting to say goodbye to the man who had raised him. He would miss him so much. He would miss the quiet words of wisdom, the sharing and the prayers. He raised his head to stare across the grave, his eyes searching the gloomy sky, thinking it matched his mood.

He turned as he was approached, taking the letter he was handed, not hearing the words spoken to him. He tucked the letter into a pocket, his head bowing once more.

He finally turned, his steps slow and heavy as he walked away. He would come back later, on another day, to say his final goodbyes. It just didn't seem real.

He slid into the vehicle waiting for him, his eyes staying on the grave until it was out of sight before he turned with a sigh, not wanting to face the empty house, the fact that he now was all alone, no one to care what he did or didn't do.

The man under the trees watched as the car moved away before he turned back to the grave. He had been successful, he thought. No one suspected anything. Now to continue with his plan. He would succeed, even if it came down to a matter of murder. It wouldn't be the first time that had been the outcome, nor would it likely be the last. A lot rested on this, he thought.

He moved away to his own car, following the young man until he entered his own home, parking his car across the street and just waiting until the lights in the house went out. Somehow, he had to make sure that his plan went forward. He would find some way to get that young man to do exactly what he wanted. His plans depended on that very fact.

He put his car in gear, driving away, an evil grin of satisfaction filling his face. Now to wait. But he only had some much patience and the men after him were not that patient.

Chapter 1

*S*itting on a bench near the centre of the little town of Mistletoe, Jacob Whitson shrugged his jacket collar higher. He had not expected it to be so busy. Nor could he understand his grandfather directing him to this town, village, he wasn't quite sure how to categorize it, or at this particular time of year. Christmas this year wouldn't be the same, not with Grand gone, he thought. It had just been the two of them for the last twelve years or so, since Gram went home. He rose, shoving his hands into his pockets, shivering against the coolness of the air. He squinted at the sky. It looked like snow, he thought, and he still had to find a place to stay. The small hotels or motels, or whatever you called them, were booked, had been for months. The proprietor at the second one had taken a look at him, went to say something, shook his head and then told him to find Finn at the local antique and used bookstore. He thought Finn might be able to help.

Lord, I have no idea why I'm here, other than Grand asked me to come in his letter. I have no idea what the journal is about. I know it's his. I recognize his handwriting. I really don't need a trip down his memory lane. I just want to pack up and move away somewhere I don't have to live with so many memories.

He stood for a moment, head tipped back, as he reached to pull his hat from his head and stick it into his pocket, his eyes on the sign of the store. Finn's Antiquities. This is it, he thought, as he reached for the old-fashioned knob on the old fashioned door, pushing it open to the sound of an old-fashioned bell. He stood, his eyes sliding closed, as he took in the smell of the building, clean but with the scent of history mingling with it. His eyes flew open as he heard a rough voice from somewhere in the back. He walked that way, a frown appearing on his face.

He stood, standing in the shadows just back from the doorway he saw led to the office at the back of the store. A roughly dressed man stood there, hands on a person Jacob couldn't see, angry words spewing from his mouth. He couldn't hear the other person's response, couldn't tell if it was a man or woman that stood there.

Jacob moved forward, knowing he couldn't stand back and let someone be assaulted. The man turned slightly at his footsteps and Jacob caught sight of the person he was threatening. A young woman, his own age, he thought. No, he could not walk away. He had to step in.

"Can I help you, ma'am?" Jacob's soft baritone broke through the angry words, causing the man to turn and glare at him.

"Butt out. This is none of your business." The man turned back to the woman. "You're coming with me. No backing out this time. You belong to me."

The young woman stood, eyes blank, not moving as the man tugged at her arm, frozen in place. Jacob drew a deep breath and then caught at the man's arm, pulling him away from the woman.

"She's not going with you, man. Now, back off. If you don't, I'm sure the police would like to hear that you're threatening someone or assaulting them."

The man swung at Jacob, who ducked the blow. He sighed to himself. He had served in the armed forces for eight years and this was nothing compared to what he had faced. He caught the man's hand and wrist and twisted it behind his back, forcing him through the building and out to the street before letting him go. He stood, facing the anger the man threw at him.

"I would suggest you leave and don't come back to bother her." Jacob watched carefully as the man finally walked away before he turned and entered the building, flipping the lock on the door and the sign to closed for now. He stood for a moment, eyeing the young woman where she still stood, unfocused.

He walked forward, gently guiding her to a chair, and then searching for water. He held the glass to her mouth, watching as she finally swallowed, the fear gradually loosening its grip on her.

She finally looked at him, a grateful look fluttering across her face. "Thank you."

Jacob crouched down in front of her. "Are you okay?" He spun slightly so he could stare at the door. "And just who was that?"

She shuddered, bringing his hand to the glass she held, taking it from her and setting it down on the desk.

"Are you sure you're okay?"

She finally nodded, her eyes clearing of the fear that had gripped her. She swallowed hard, knowing she had to explain.

Jacob stood, his hand raised. "Don't explain if you don't want to. I'm a stranger here." He looked back at the store. "I was sent here to talk to Finn."

"I'm Finn. Who sent you?" She stood, walking through to the counter in the store, frowning at the sign on the door, her words causing Jacob to spin and stare at her.

"The man in the small hotel near the downtown. I'm looking for somewhere to stay and all the rooms are taken. He seemed to think you might be able to help." Jacob withdrew his keys from his pockets. "It's okay. I don't need to stay here in town."

"No, that's okay. This has just shaken me. Before I forget, thank you for stepping in. No one else in town would have. He's a bully, used to getting what he wants."

"What did he mean, then, that you belong to him, if you don't mind my asking?" Jacob watched as Finn grimaced, her hand rubbing at her wrist.

"He thinks I'm his, that whatever he says I'll do. He's been told to stay away. I have a restraining order against him, for all the good it does."

"He should stay away, then. Why don't the police get involved?"

She snorted in a very unladylike manner. "Because the police chief is his father and according to him, Gerry can do and does not do any wrong. It's always the other person's fault. I had to fight to get a restraining order, going to the judge myself. I'm not the first one to seek one against him. He backs off if he finds out a lady he's harassing gets herself a boyfriend or husband."

"Well, then, I'm Jacob Whitson. Happy to meet you and I would be glad to stand in as a substitute friend if you need it." His deep gray eyes sparkled with mischief as he reached to push back a lock of deep red curls that had dropped over his forehead, taking in the amber eyes and golden hair of the lady standing in front of him.

She shook her head at him. "Really? I might just take you up on that. Seeing as you've locked me up for the day, just let me ring off the cash, stick it in the safe, and I'll take you to my parents' B&B. I know they still have a room there." She paused, looking at him in a strange manner. "Have you ever been here before?"

He shook his head. "No, I haven't. My grandfather died about three months ago and his last request was that I come here during December and search for something he's hidden in a journal. He used to live here when he was a teenager."

"What was his name?"

"Aaron Whitson." He watched her reaction, not expecting it.

"Aaron? Oh, my! He was a friend of my grandfather. Pops used to talk about him a lot, wondering where he was and how he was."

She soon had led him through town to her parents' home, his car following closely behind hers. He stood for a moment at the bottom of the wooden stairs, staring up at the two-story sprawling wood clad house, feeling like he had come home. A sense of danger and adventure coursed through him. Lord, I've come home, I think, but I feel the danger out there. We need your protection, both Finn and I.

Chapter 2

Finn pointed to the closet where she had hung her jacket and set her shoes, waiting for him to do the same, before leading him towards the back of the house. He hesitated, knowing he was a guest and knowing she was heading for their personal quarters.

She turned, frowning as he hadn't followed her. "Jacob? Come on. Mom's here in the kitchen." When he still didn't move, she caught his arm, pulling him with her. "You're not a guest, Jacob. You're a friend. Friends are allowed back here." She threw him a grin as she pushed through a door. "Mom?"

"In the kitchen, love. You're home early. No trouble, I hope."

"Yeah, well, that's a story for another day." Finn hugged her mother.

"Not again, Finn. When will he leave you alone?" She didn't look up from where she was working at the counter.

Finn shrugged. "I have no idea. I don't think he ever will, Mom." She looked up at Jacob, over her mother's bent head, and shook her head. "Mom, I brought home someone I think you'll be interested in meeting."

Finn's mother, Mary, looked up from the cookies she was icing at that, seeing for the first time Jacob standing there. Her hands froze for a moment before she dropped the icing bag and came around the counter, wiping her hands on a damp towel as she did so.

"Aaron?"

Jacob shook his head. "Jacob. Aaron was my grandfather."

"You look so much like a photo Timothy Sr. has of the two of them." She reached to hug him, surprising him.

Jacob gave a small smile. "That's what they tell me."

Mary turned to frown at her daughter. "And just how does Jacob fit in to what happened?"

Finn sighed, knowing she'd have to confess. "He walked in on it. John sent him to me to see if we had a room for him."

"Of course we do. He can have Dad's room. It's empty and and I know Dad would have liked to have met his friend's grandson. Where's your luggage, Jacob?" She turned back to face him, studying his face.

Jacob stared at her, not quite sure of what had just happened, but feeling that he had been welcomed home. "It's, uh, it's in my car, out front."

"That's fine, then. Finn, get your chocolate out and make you both some. I just have to finish these for the guests' tea and I can join you." Mary bustled away, leaving Jacob staring after her, feeling as if he had been caught in a whirlwind.

Finn laughed. "She's always like that, Jacob. Better get used to it." She pointed at a sitting area off to the side. "Have a seat in there and I'll be right with you. You do drink hot chocolate, don't you?"

He shook his head. "No, actually, I don't. I never have acquired the taste for it."

"What will you have then? Coffee, tea, hot cider, or something cold?"

"Tea sounds good." He grinned. "How many flavours do I get to choose from?"

"About a dozen. If you've no real preference, I like English tea."

"That sounds wonderful. Thank you." He waited, taking the tray from her and watching until she had seated herself. "Now, about today."

She frowned at him, then paused to sip her tea, gathering her thoughts. "What about today?"

"Just what I asked." His eyes watched her intently, so intent she shifted in her chair. "Does he come around a lot?"

She shook her head. "Not really. Although in the last couple of weeks, I've seen him watching me from a distance and walking back and forth in front of the store. Today was the first time he has approached like that in a long time."

"What would have happened had I not been there?"

She shuddered. "I have no idea, Jacob, and I don't even want to think about it."

He nodded, his eyes watchful, his thoughts turning into a prayer for his new friend. He looked up as he heard a commotion from the front of the house.

Finn sighed as she set her cup down on its saucer and rose. "I just knew he'd show up sooner or later."

"Who?" Jacob rose as well, his hand reaching automatically for his phone and turning on the video recorder. It was a habit he had in certain circumstances, and he felt this was one of those. He set his phone down, propped up against his mug, even as a large man stalked through the doors from the front of the house, a belligerent attitude flowing from him.

"What's the meaning of this, Finn? What did you do to Gerry?" The venom and hatred towards Finn spewed from him.

She snorted. "I did nothing to him. He did it to himself."

"Right. Sure he did. He said he was attacked and hurt." The man's eyes never left Finn's face.

Jacob eased up behind her, reaching to envelope her in his arms, crossing his around her just below her own that she had folded across her body. Finn tensed for a moment, then relaxed subtly, enough that she leaned back against Jacob. His arms tightened just enough that she felt the strength of his character in how he held her.

The man shook his head. "I know you, Finn. I know you did something to him. You've always lied about him."

Finn stared at him, her mouth slightly open. "Really? After all the complaints that went in to the department, that were never followed up on? Not just by me, either. The ladies in this town know the character of Gerry. It's his family that doesn't recognize it."

Jacob watched the darkness settle deeper on the man's face and sighed inwardly. What did you just go and do, Finn? Why did you say that? And just who is this man?

Finn shifted her weight closer to Jacob even as he watched the man approach closer. His eyes lifted to the man entering quietly from the front of the house, catching a glimpse of Mary coming in from the dining room, and vague movement of a younger man entering through the back door. His focus returned to Finn and the man standing in front of her.

"All lies, Finn. All lies. You know that."

Finn shook her head. "And you know they're not." She drew in a sharp breath as she watched the man's hands clench into fists. With that, Jacob had released her and swept her behind him.

"I think you should leave now, before you do something you regret." Jacob's words were soft but forceful, drawing the man's attention to himself.

"Stay out of this. This doesn't concern you."

"On the contrary, it does. I will not stay by and watch a lady of any age bullied."

Jacob's words drew the man's focus totally to him. Anger and another emotion Jacob couldn't define crossed his face and then the man's fist was heading for Jacob's face. Jacob felt the force of the blow he didn't have time to duck, the force driving him backwards and down into darkness. His backward motion caught Finn and took her down with him, their bodies hitting the floor in a solid thud. The younger man sprang froward, his stance protective as he stood in front of them.

Timothy Bronagh sprang forward as well, his hand going to the police chief's arm to prevent further blows being lodged on their guest. He wasn't in time to prevent the heavy kick the man launched at Jacob.

"George. Enough of this. You've gone too far this time. When this gets reported to the council, you'll be done."

George spun, almost spitting in Timothy's face in his rage. "It will be my word against yours. I always win."

"Not this time, George. Not this time. You entered a private residence without cause or a warrant. You've assaulted someone without provocation. No, this time you're done. Now leave." Timothy swept his arm towards the door, one eye on the man, the other trying to assess the two on the floor.

"This isn't over, not by a long shot. If he stays in town, he will be arrested for assault on Gerry."

Timothy shook his head in a sorrowful manner. "I don't think so, George. Your time of running the town is over, I think. Not with who you just assaulted."

George Adams scoffed. "He's just a stranger in town. What's the big deal?"

"He's more than just a stranger, George. I understand that's Jacob Whitson, Aaron's grandson."

George's face whitened as his mouth opened and closed, his lips unable to form words. He finally spun, his footsteps heavy and hurried.

Mary rushed forward, dropping to her knees beside the young couple even as Finn struggled to sit up, her brother's hands reaching for her.

"Finn? Are you okay?" Timothy crouched beside them, his eyes on his daughter.

"I am, Dad. Jacob?" Her eyes flew to him, her heart in her throat at the thought of how he had been injured stepping in front of her.

Jacob rolled to his back, his eyes flickering open and closed. "My phone!"

Peter's eyes flew to where the phone sat and he frowned even as he reached for it. "Jacob? Your phone? At a time like this?"

Jacob nodded, regretting it as pain spread through his face and head. "Video."

Peter's eyes brightened as comprehension dawned. "Wonderful! We have proof we can take somewhere."

Finn stared between the two men even as she heard quiet footsteps approaching the door and saw her father rising to greet one of their guests who stood there. "What's so important about his phone?"

"He has a video of what just happened, Finn. We have proof. It's timestamped and everything."

Jacob's eyes slid shut against the pain. "A habit I have." His words were mumbled as he fought to stay conscious.

Timothy stared at his guest, wondering that he had come into their private quarters. Then his face cleared at the man's words.

"I don't want to intrude, but I was in the lounge and heard what was said. I was a medic in the armed forces. May I take a look?" The younger man's eyes drifted past Timothy and lit on Jacob, a sound of recognition pulled from him.

"Whit?" He too dropped down beside Jacob, his hands reaching to assess him.

Jacob pulled himself back from the blackness he was drifting into. "Blackie? What are you doing here?"

"I'm moving to this town. I thought it would be a nice quiet town." Levi Blackwell stared down at his friend, concern on his face even as he grinned. "At least it was until you showed up. And that's something we need to talk about. But first. How's the head?" Long fingers gently probed at Jacob's jaw and head, before Blackie turned his attention to Finn. "Are you all right?"

She nodded. "I just had the breath knocked out of me for a bit. How is Jacob?"

Blackie reached down a hand to pull Jacob to his feet, a hand steadying his friend before he guided him to a chair. "He's fine. He's got a hard head."

Timothy and Mary exchanged glances before Mary spoke. "But you seem to know Jacob. How?"

"We served together, Ma'am. I lost track of him when we both left the service." He studied his friend. "There have been a couple of other friends looking for him. Something has drawn us to this area."

Jacob stared at his friend, eyes narrowed, knowing they would have to talk and that there was something Blackie wasn't saying. "We'll talk." Jacob's attention turned Finn. "Are you okay, Finn?"

She nodded. "Don't ever do that again, Jacob. Don't ever step in front of me like that." She glared at her brother as he snickered.

Jacob stared at her without blinking, until she looked down. "Don't even think I won't, Finn. I won't let any man bully a lady, not if I can help it." He looked around at the five staring at him. "What's his problem, anyway?"

Timothy sighed as he accepted the mug of coffee his wife handed him before he too sat in one of the arm chairs. "He's pretty much run the town for years now. We've had issues with him, but the council is running scared of him and his bullies. Any recruit we get to the force that is decent moves on within a short period of time."

"Toxic." Blackie spoke up.

Timothy's head swung his way as he frowned. "Toxic? That's a good way to describe it. We've gone to the next level of law enforcement but he's always been able to talk his way out of anything. But you, Jacob. You've come here for a reason." Timothy pointed to the younger man. "I have no idea what brought you here, other than God."

Jacob shrugged. "I never knew this town existed, not really. Grand never talked about when he was real young. I was handed his journal and a letter from him at his grave, but I had no intention of coming here, even though he asked me to. His lawyer finally convinced me I needed to, to come find "my roots" as he put it. I haven't read the letter yet and only glanced through the journal, just enough to find the name of this town."

The four Bronaghs exchanged glances before Mary spoke. "Then, you really have no ideas of what this town means to you."

Jacob shook his head, a sudden dread filling him. *Lord, what did I go and walk into? I have a feeling I'm in over my head right now. I really really need Your strength and guidance right now.*

Timothy sighed as he stared at his wife, waiting before she gave a reluctant nod. "Then, let me fill you in on what this town means to you. First, Mary, let's dish up our dinner. Blackie, may I call you that?" At his nod, Timothy continued. "Please, join us. A friend of Jacob's is a friend of ours. We need to talk. Then, Jacob has some decisions he'll need to make. One, I hope, is going to the next level of law enforcement with his video."

"Next level? As in the county police?" Blackie suddenly grinned, drawing frowns from those watching him. "Jacob, Simon's on the county force. You'll have someone who'll believe you."

"Simon? Oh, that's wonderful." Jacob set his fork on his plate, the casserole there forgotten for the moment, arms resting on the table as his eyes sought Finn, watching her for a moment, unaware of the interest he was garnering. "Timothy, what was it you had to say?" His attention turned to Timothy.

Timothy sat back, folding his arms across his chest, as he studied the younger man. "Your great great grandfather founded this town, along with my great grandfather. Your roots run deep here, son, deeper than you know. I'm glad you're back. I wish Aaron had come back to stay. He was in and out the last couple of years, here for a couple of hours and then gone. We never had a chance to speak. But I do know this. Your grandfather owned about half the buildings in this town. If he passed his estate on to you, then you now own those buildings. That would be why you were pushed to come here."

Chapter 3

$\mathcal{J}$acob lay in bed late that night, his eyes on the white of the moonlight as it filtered through the window sheers and reflected in the mirror of the antique dresser on the opposite wall. He shivered, not from the cold, but from the coming difficulties he sensed he faced. He rolled over, pulling the blankets up around his ears, trying to find the sleep that eluded him. He sighed, knowing he wouldn't get much sleep that night. His thoughts turned to the events of earlier, and he frowned. How had the police chief gotten away with so much for so many years?

Then his thought drifted to his grandfather. Grand, was this what you wanted to talk to me about that night? You were gone, graduated to heaven, so quickly that day, I never got to say good bye to you. He wiped at the tears that wet his face. It had been just him and Grand for so many years after his Grams went. He had been a young teenager. Grand hadn't wanted him to join the forces, but hadn't stood in his way, pride in him reflecting every time he saw his Grand after that. They had taken him in after his parents had been killed in a typhoon serving overseas as missionaries.

He rolled over again, restless with his thoughts. He had never imagined his grandfather owned so much property. He had never said, never talked about finances at all with him. He wished he had. Then he would have been better prepared to hear what Timothy had told him. He sighed, his heart turning to prayer. Lord, I have no idea where this is going. I am so over my head in this situation, even more than when I had to arrest a fellow soldier. I never wanted to be an MP but that's what You chose for me. Guide us here, Lord.

He finally drifted off, his thoughts on Finn, a smile on his face. He knew without a shadow of a doubt he wanted to spend time with her. He prayed for his new friends, not knowing just how much those prayers would be needed in the coming days. He felt the sense of doom approaching, but ignored it.

Finn stirred in the early morning light, her eyes opening to the early winter morning. She squinted at the clock and sighed. There would be no more sleep for her. Today was a big day in their town - annual Christmas festivities starting during the morning. She still had to finish her decorations outside her store.

She pushed back the covers and swung her feet out of the bed, stopping as she saw the bruising on her wrist. Jacob had noticed it the previous night when her sweater sleeve had pulled back and insisted Blackie check it out before he took pictures of it. She tried to get him not to but he just shook his head and continued. *Lord, I have no idea who he is or what he's here for, but I sense that You brought him here. Protect him please.*

She paused as she pulled the soft jade sweater over her head, a frown appearing. *Lord, Jacob's here and I just know he's going to change things in this town. I just know he's going to change things for me.* She drew a deep breath, realizing finally that she had let him encircle her with his arms, holding her against him, and she had let him. In fact, she had moved backwards against him, into the strength of his body and character. This was not her. Not since the attack so many years ago when she had been beaten by a high school acquaintance. She hadn't let any male touch her, just her father and brother. She stared at her image in the mirror. *Lord, am I finally healing?*

She greeted her mother, grabbing her tea to go and her usual bagel, and headed for the street. She usually walked to work if she could. Today, she needed that time alone just to try and figure out her feelings. And somehow, she didn't think the fifteen minute walk would work.

She stood for a moment staring at the town centre, the large pine tree with the lights ready for the lighting ceremony that night. She spun in a circle, studying the other businesses in the square, noting she was the only one not yet ready. She sighed. This year, she hadn't been in the mood to decorate, even though she knew she had to. Some years, she despaired of ever finding the spirit she needed for that time of year and quite often not finding it.

She shoved open her shop door and headed for the office, dropping her purse into the usual drawer and locking it.

She dug around to find the decorations, standing back and staring at them. She put the same ones up year after year, just because it's what her Pops had done with the shop.

She sighed and turned to the front of the store as she heard the bell. It had to be a visitor to town, she thought. Townspeople never came in that early. She stopped, her eyes on Jacob as he laid a journal on the counter, then turned to study the shop, moving quietly and slowly through it before he ended up in front of the door, his eyes meeting hers before a smile lit his face.

"Finn! I didn't see you standing there." He turned back, his arm sweeping around the view of the store. "I like this store. Your mom said it used to be your grandfather's?"

"It was. I grew up in here with him. He taught me what I knew, sent me to study with experts and paid for college courses for me. We shared the same love of the old." She moved towards him. "You're out and about early."

"Habit." He grinned at her. "I got used to being up and about early in the armed forces and can't shake the habit." He followed her back into the office as she shook her head. "Your mom said you had to decorate your shop. Let me help."

She finally nodded, a pensive look on her face. "I've done it on my own for the last few years, since Pops went. It's not the same."

Jacob froze for a moment, realizing how true it was. This would be the first year without any of his own people. "It's true."

She turned, catching the momentary look of sadness of his face, before he smiled.

"These boxes are the ones you're working from?" At her nod, he gathered up some and headed for the front of the store. "Where do we start, inside or outside? And do you have to do the same thing every year?"

She started to laugh. "Inside, and no. Why? Do you have fresh ideas?"

He grinned as he nodded and then opening the boxes, starting going through them. "Oh, this is wonderful. I have so many ideas. You shouldn't let me loose, you know."

"All I can say is go for it. I'm glad for some fresh ideas. I don't have the heart to change what Pops always did."

"I don't want to offend anyone, Finn. If it will, I won't go ahead with any of my ideas."

She shook her head even as she laid a hand on his arm, her eyes focused on that movement. He's changing me already, Lord. I'm not sure I'm ready for this but as long as You're not saying no or stopping me, I'll go along with it. "No. It's time I changed things and made it my own. Rather, your own."

Two hours later, Finn stepped back to the edge of the sidewalk to study the decorations outside the store, her face flushed with laughter, Jacob grinning at her unrepentantly. Her parents watched from the other side of the street, smiles on their faces.

"He's good for our Finn, Mary." Timothy sighed inwardly, knowing her happiness might not last.

"He is. I haven't seen her that happy or laughing so hard since before her attack. I pray he stays here."

"That's all we can do, dear. Dad would have liked him."

"That he would have. I wish he could have met him." Mary drew in a deep breath as she saw the officer approaching Finn. "Not now, please."

Timothy's hand tightened on his wife's. "Jacob will look after her. Trust him."

Finn looked up as she heard her name, freezing momentarily as she saw the police uniform, not hearing Jacob call to her or feel him moving behind her, an arm coming around her.

The officer, a friend of Peter's, stood for a moment watching the two, his eyes thoughtful. He had heard from Peter what had happened the night before and had promised he'd watch out for Finn, a lady he considered a sister. His eyes searched Jacob's before he nodded.

"I had a complaint there was too much fun going on here, Finn." He grinned as she shook a finger at him.

"And who complained? Peter?" She leaned back on Jacob, not realizing she was doing that, drawing Tom's eyes to the movement. "Tom, this is Jacob Whitson. You've heard of Aaron? This is his grandson.

Tom reached to shake Jacob's hand. "Welcome to your town, Jacob. Sorry the welcome wasn't so good last night." He looked around. "Watch your backs, you two." He moved past them, his eyes watching the crowds.

Jacob watched him walk away before his own eyes searched the crowds and before he looked down at the lady he still held and who hadn't made any move to step away from him. He liked the feeling of her in his arms.

She tilted her eyes to search his face before she moved out of his arms, her eyes back on the building.

"I like what you've done, Jacob. This is so unique and so true to what we have inside." He had used her grandfather's decorations in a different way and they had been getting compliments from the neighbouring businesses.

"I'm glad." He stepped back towards the curb with her, his eyes assessing what they had done. "Your work in the window helps. I like how you've used objects from the kitchen to make believe you're cooking an old-fashioned dinner."

She laughed, something she had done a lot of that day. Something about Jacob had released the lock on her emotions and her heart and she finally felt free of what had held her back. She felt a sudden shove and screamed, finding herself falling towards the street and the oncoming traffic. There was no way she could avoid being run down.

Jacob, hearing her scream, spun, his hands and arms reaching for her and cradling her to him even as his feet shoved him away from the street. He hit the sidewalk with a heavy thud, protecting Finn as much as he could, rolling towards the building even as the pedestrians scattered around them and ran, a few heading their way to help.

Tom dropped to his knees beside them, even as he reached for his radio. He knew the call would go nowhere, the chief would make sure of that once he knew who was involved. He frowned. There had been something different about the chief as he walked through the building that morning. He wasn't as arrogant in his manner as he usually was and he didn't stop to berate any of the men and women milling around during the shift change.

"Finn? Jacob?" Tom reached to help entangle the two, the man from the neighbouring bakeshop on his knees to help.

"Finn was pushed, Tom." Ed's words were breathless. "If it weren't for this young man, she'd have been under someone's tires."

Jacob pushed back Finn's hair even as they sat up on the sidewalk, his hand resting for a moment on her cheek. "You're okay? You're not hurt? I tried to protect you."

Finn's eyes were wide and frightened before she took a deep breath and then slapped Jacob's shoulder. "You have to stop doing that, Jacob. You'll be killed next time." She shoved to her feet and stormed through her store door, the door banging shut behind her.

Jacob stood, hands shoved into his jacket pockets, as he watched before he felt Tom's hand on his shoulder.

"Give her a moment. She reacts like this when she's scared. She gets mad." Tom looked around. "No one will have seen anything. I can guarantee you that. I'll ask the normal questions and that will be the answer I get."

Jacob nodded, even as he watched the crowd once more hurrying by them, the excitement over. "What's really going on, Tom? She shouldn't be treated like this, not in a town called Mistletoe."

"No, no one should, but the chief has made it clear that she is persona non gratis, because of his son. We've tried to talk to him and usually end up with a report on our file because of it. Those of us who are loyal to our people and town have made a pact to protect the people the chief has taken a dislike to." He paused, searching for the right words. "And you'll be at the top of his list. Peter talked to me last night. Watch your back." He nodded towards the door. "Watch Finn. She's letting you do things no one else can. I saw her back up to you when I approached. She's never done that before. Never let any male other than her family touch her. She's let you. For some reason, the trust is there before she really knows you. Don't break it."

Jacob nodded. "I won't. I think it goes back to our grandfathers being friends. She may feel like she knows me."

Tom stared at him for a moment, then shook his head. "That's not it, Jacob. You have a presence about you, a presence that demands respect. You can intimidate if you have to. I hear tell you did that last night. We need you in this town." He nodded towards Finn's store. "She needs you in her life, Jacob, whether or not she realizes it. And not just to stop what's been going for years, something none of us have been able to stop or even figure out what it is." He slapped Jacob on the shoulder before walking away.

"He's right, you know?" Jacob spun at the voice behind him. Ed stood there. "I've had my shop next to this one for as long as Finn can remember and even longer. She's never reacted to someone like she has to you. I haven't heard her laugh like she was and for her to giggle like she was? No one has heard that since she was a young child. Stick around. I knew your grandpa. You look like him and it appears that you act just like him."

Jacob stared, openmouthed, after him as he walked back into his store even as he heard the bell jingle at Finn's. She stood there, eyes on him.

"Well, get in here already, will you? I have your tea ready for you. Ed sent over some sweets for us. Then I need to check my online orders while you research your journal." She watched with sympathy as he froze beside her at those words. A hand was laid on his arm. "He would want you to read it here in Mistletoe, Jacob. This was his hangout when he was young, this store. It isn't what it was then, but he and Pops hung around here with my great grandparents."

He stood, nodding his head, willing the tears back down. He couldn't and swiped angrily at the ones that escaped to roll down his cheeks. He heard a soft sound from Finn before she drew him into the store and hand wrapped around his arm, back to the office where she turned to him and hugged him. He stood for a moment before his arms reached around her and his head rested on hers, accepting the comfort she was giving. He finally released her, not looking at her for a moment. When he did, he saw the tears sparkling in her own eyes. He reached to trace the track of one that had escaped.

"Thank you."

She nodded, then pointed to the chair he had used the day before. "Sit before our tea gets cold."

He watched as she worked away at her computer, rising every once in a while to help a customer. He wandered through the shop, his eyes drawn to the books and journals she had on display. He frowned for a moment as he reached for one.

Finn watched from where she was gift wrapping an old small globe for a tourist, her attention wavering for a moment, before it returned to her customer. She smiled at the man's thanks and watched as he walked away. It would soon be closing time, but then the festivities in the square would begin. This year, she just didn't want to be in a crowd. She didn't feel safe, even though it was her town.

She walked over to where Jacob stood. "What did you find, Jacob?"

"This." He help up the journal. "It's got a cover like Grand's." He carefully opened it, a frown on his face. "This is strange. This is Grams' handwriting. How did it end up here?"

Finn shook her head. "I think I took that in with a bunch of books someone found in a house they were renting. They were told they could clear out the attic and get rid of anything they didn't want." She paused, her eyes shifting to stare into the distance. "I think it was a house your grandfather owned." She placed a hand on his, finding his shaking, and closed her fingers around his. "It might have been your grandfather's house. Mom or Dad will know. But I"m not even sure that's how it got here." She reached for it. "Come to think of it, I don't remember seeing it before."

He nodded, a somber look on his face. "I need to buy this from you, Finn. I need to read through both of these. Maybe it will give me answers as to why Grand wanted me to come here."

He looked up at her as her fingers tightened on his and frowned, a puzzled look on his face, his eyes searching hers. Lord, what is it about this lady that draws me when no other one ever did? Guide me here, please. I don't want to hurt this lady, not at all.

"It's yours, Jacob. I can't charge you for something that belongs to your family." She shook her head as he opened his mouth to protest, a finger laid across his lips. "No. It's yours. It should have always been. I'm not sure why your grandmother didn't have it with her or how it got here. She wasn't from here, not that I know of."

He shook his head. "No, she wasn't. I wonder." He stared down at the journal, a distant look in his eyes. "Grand disappeared for a couple of days after Grams died. Maybe he came back here and left it here." He sighed. "I suddenly feel like I'm caught in a whirlwind or something, that I'm lost on some path where I can't see around the bend." He glanced at the clock. "Your mother's expecting us for dinner before we come back here. Let me help you lock up for the night." He stacked the two journals together with his coat.

Chapter 4

$\mathscr{T}$ightening her jade patterned scarf around her neck, Finn dug into her pocket for her gloves. With the sun going down, it was getting chilly. Snow flakes drifted lazily down and she tilted her face to feel them caress her skin. Jacob smiled at the picture she make, not aware of how her parents were watching and then exchanging their own smiles. He reached for her hand, surprising her. She stared at their linked hands before she shrugged and followed as he tugged her towards the downtown.

Jacob led Finn among her fellow townspeople and the visitors, finding just the right spot to watch the activities where they would be sheltered and out of sight.

"Will this do?" Jacob smiled down at Finn as she glanced around.

"Perfect. It's my favourite spot for watching the festivities but I don't often get it." She reached up to drop a kiss on his cheek. "Thank you."

Jacob stood, his eyes on her as she looked around the crowd, waving to friends. He wanted to touch the spot, but didn't. He sighed to himself. He had no intention of living in a small town, but he also had no intention of living in the town he grew up in. He searched the crowd, seeing people who had approached him over the course of the day, talking about his grandfather and his ancestors. He was drawn here but he just didn't know.

Movement to his side caught his eye and he turned, a frown on his face that smoothed out when he saw Blackie standing back from him, watching the crowd. He looked past him as the man standing next to Blackie nodded at him. He grinned suddenly. Simon was there. Now, where was Joshua? A movement to his other side had his head turning that way. Joshua. Joshua nodded before his eyes dropped to Finn and then back up. Jacob's heart stilled as he got the message. Something was up tonight that involved Finn and his friends had picked up for him.

Finn turned at that point, her eyes on his face, a smile on her face. She seemed relaxed, more than he had seen in the couple of days since he met her.

"Thank you, Jacob."

“For what?”

“For being who you are. You’re like what Pops always said your grandfather was like.”

He hugged her at that, tears prickling at his eyes, tears he willed back down. “Thank you for saying that. He was a wonderful man. Sure, he had his faults, who doesn’t? But he stayed true to his course and that was being a man of God.”

They turned back to the square, watching as the festivities started, listening to the local band playing the carols and Christmas songs, the cheers as the tree was lighted, the oohs and ahs from the children as they watched the lights flicker to life on the tree.

Jacob finally pushed away from the wall, his hand catching Finn’s as they moved through the crowd.

“What happens now?”

She shrugged. “People stay here, mingling meeting old and new friends. A service club serves hot drinks. Another one hands out candy canes to all the kids.”

He nodded, his eyes searching for his friends and not seeing them. That didn’t worry him, he knew they were with them.

"Jacob?" He looked down as she said his name. "You seem distracted tonight."

He shook his head. "Not really, although you are a distraction, one of the nice ones." He laughed as she blushed. "My friends are here somewhere, and I was hoping to introduce you to both Simon and Joshua."

"Joshua?" She mulled over the name. "Is he a cook by chance?"

Jacob nodded. "He was. I'm not sure what he's up to now. We lost track of one another when we left the armed forces."

"There's a new cafe in town called The House. The owner's name is Josh. Would that be him?"

He nodded. "It would be. I'll need to check it out next week. Knowing Josh, it won't be open on Sundays."

She agreed. "He's been here for about a year, I think. He's been pressured to open on Sundays. The police chief has been one of the ones after him. He has refused."

Jacob sighed. "Is there nothing that man isn't involved in or won't do?"

"Not much." She turned as she heard running footsteps approaching them.

A hand went across her mouth as an arm swung around her, trapping her arms as she was picked up. She heard a sound from Jacob and then was out of his sight, carried through a back alley to a vehicle. Her hands were bound behind her and a gag tightened over her mouth before she was dumped into a trunk. She heard murmured words and then felt the car shift as someone sat in it. She felt the movement as the car moved away. Her heart sank. Who had taken her and why? She had a good idea who was behind it but without proof no one would ever believe her.

She felt desperately around the trunk, trying to find a weapon or something to release her bonds and found nothing. She stared at the lights, and then raising a foot, kicked at one of the lights, finally breaking the plastic. Cold air rushed in and she shivered.

Maybe that wasn't such a good idea after all, she thought. I'm going to freeze to death. Lord, help me. She laid her head down, too stressed to cry, too worried about Jacob.

Jacob struggled to sit up, Blackie's arm around his shoulder holding him upright. The blow had caught him in his back, at the site of an old injury that still plagued him. The sudden pain had sent him down to his knees even as Finn's hand was ripped from his.

"Finn?" His breath came in gasps as he tried to control his pain.

Blackie looked around. "She's not here, Whit. Simon and Josh are after her. We weren't close enough to stop it." He looked down at his friend, before reaching down a hand to pull him to his feet. "I'm sorry."

Jacob leaned against the wall behind him. "This was planned, Blackie. For some reason. I think you'll find the police chief and his son are somehow behind it, though why I have no idea."

Blackie looked around, saw an officer approaching them and hand on Jacob's arm, drew him down an alley where he stuffed him into his truck. "I don't think you want to talk to the police in this town."

Jacob shook his head, his breath finally evening out as the pain subsided. "Not really. I know there are good ones, Tom for one, but I can't be sure even about him."

Blackie pulled his phone out. "Josh says they're on the trail of the car." He started to laugh. "Your lady's good, Jacob. Josh said it looked as if there's a light out on the back. Would she have known to kick it out?"

"I have no idea, Blackie. I just met her yesterday. Our grandfathers were friends, but other than that, I don't know of any connection to her." His eyes searched the vehicles ahead of them, not knowing which one was Simon's and not knowing which one held Finn.

Blackie stared at Jacob for a few seconds before his eyes returned to the road ahead of him. He couldn't believe that. Those two have a connection like I've never seen. Lord, protect Jacob's lady, whatever it is she is involved with. Guide us to her tonight.

Josh read the text he had received from Blackie. "They're behind us, somewhere, Simon. Are we following the right car?"

Simon Gardner nodded. "We are. I had my eye on that car earlier. The way it was parked just shouted something was off about it. I don't trust the police in Mistletoe enough to alert them."

Joshua Smithson nodded. "I know there are some good cops there. I've met them. But their hands are basically tied by the chief. We need to get him out of there."

Simon pointed. "There. That's our car. What on earth?" He started to laugh. "She's kicked out a light by the looks of it."

Josh stared at Simon for a moment before he looked back at the car. "Smart lady. She's a good match for Whit." He stared around. "Hey! Didn't we just leave the town?"

Simon nodded, a grim look on his face as he reached for his phone. "We did. We can arrest him now, whoever he is, and charge him in our county. He won't get away with kidnapping in our jurisdiction. My boss has been looking for information and evidence on the chief in Mistletoe for years."

"Blackie said Whit taped what happened last night. You know Whit. He set up a video recording when the chief entered their private residence."

"He did? Wonderful. David will be so glad to hear that. We need to get it from Whit."

"We do." He watched as the car ahead swerved across the road and back. "What is he doing?"

"I have no idea." Simon stared ahead. "I can see the lights from the county force heading our way. We'll trap him between us.

There are no roads or lanes he can turn off onto in this stretch." Then his breath caught and he slammed on his brakes. "He really didn't just go and do that, did he?"

"He did." Josh had his seatbelt off and was out of the truck, heading for the car.

The kidnapper had spun his wheel when he realized he was trapped, sending the car trunk first into the trees. The two men running that way winced at the sound of metal crumpling. They slid to a stop, taking a look at the driver before heading for the trunk, their hearts sinking as they saw it crumpled badly.

"Watch him, Josh." Simon ran for his truck, flagging down the patrol officer responding to his call for help. The officer nodded, reaching back in for his radio.

Simon grabbed his tire iron and another pry bar he had dropped into the tool box just by chance. He stared at it for a moment. No, he thought, it was not just by chance. It was God.

He slid to a halt beside Josh, who was frantically trying to open the trunk, handing him the pry bar. Together, the two men worked feverishly to free the twisted metal without success. Simon looked up as he heard the sirens and then the sound of a diesel engine. He stepped back, pulling Josh with him as the firefighters ran their way, dragging the equipment they needed.

Josh looked up as he heard another vehicle stop. "It's Whit. Let me go see him."

Simon nodded as he cast a look that way before watching the crumpled metal give way. He drew closer as the paramedics traded places with the firefighters and worked on Finn.

"Is she alive?" Simon could barely ask the question.

"She is, and I don't know how." The paramedic shot a glance around the trunk. "The way it crumpled, that saved her. She was thrown forward against the back seat when the trunk crumpled from the top back."

Simon nodded, then turned to make his way towards Jacob, Blackie, and Josh. He could feel the tension and anguish radiating from Jacob before he reached him

Jacob shot him a look and then turned to watch where the paramedics were working on Finn.

"Jacob." Simon sighed. "Jacob!" His voice raised a bit and Jacob jumped and turned to him.

"She's alive, Whit. Somehow, she's alive. She's unconscious, which is not unexpected. They'll be transporting her soon." He watched the relief flood over Jacob before he shared a look with their two friends. "I have a patrol officer on his way to find her parents and her brother, I think Blackie said?"

"Peter. Please." Jacob walked rapidly away from them towards the ambulance. A few quick words and he was on board, watching Finn's face intently.

"Is that really Whit?" Josh's voice was quiet. "And you said Finn?" At Blackie's nod, he continued. "I know Finn from town and from church. I didn't realize Whit knew her as well."

"Not until last night." Blackie filled the two in on what had transpired. "I think he's smitten, whether he realizes it or not."

Josh nodded, a thought crossing his mind. "Did you say he hugged her last night and then was holding her hand tonight?" He grinned suddenly. "She doesn't let any male that close to her, except her brother and father. I think Whit has himself a lady."

The two other men shook their heads. Blackie then spoke. "I'll head in to the hospital. Josh, you with me?"

"No, I'll stay with Simon. I think I have to give a statement or something like that."

Blackie nodded as he walked back to his vehicle, his heart raised in prayer for his friend's lady. He searched the traffic stopped by the accident, his eyes zeroing in on a certain truck. He pulled out his phone and took a photo, making sure he took one of the plate, before he slid behind the wheel and pulled away, being waved through the scene.

❀ ❀ ❀ ❀ ❀

Two hours later, Jacob looked up and then stood as he found Mary standing in front of him, Timothy and Peter flanking her. She reached to hug him, then sat beside him, his hand in both of hers.

"Mary. Timothy. I'm sorry."

Timothy shook his head. "Not your fault, Jacob. He would have taken her no matter who she was with. At least you were there and because you were, your friends were and found her so quickly." He leaned back in the chair, his eyes sliding closed. "Thank God you were all there." His eyes opened as he assessed the younger man before he nodded. "Finn has let you into her life in a way she has never let anyone else, not even us. I know you'll be careful with her."

"I will." Jacob looked up as he heard footsteps. "Any word on her condition?"

"She's conscious. They're running some more tests and want to keep her overnight but I'm not sure they'll win that battle."

Jacob nodded. "If she goes home, Blackie can check on her for you." Blackie nodded his agreement from where he stood close to them.

Jacob excused himself, walking towards his three friends. "Simon. Josh. It's so good to see you two again." He reached to hug his friends.

"And you." Josh looked around. "Is there somewhere we can grab a coffee? We need to talk, Jacob, and not in front of her people."

Jacob shot a look backwards and then shrugged. "I have no idea, Josh. Simon?"

"There a little cafe just around the corner. We can go there. Just let me speak to her people and I'll catch up."

Jacob looked at his friends over his coffee cup, seeing the grim looks on their faces and sighed to himself. This was not the way he hoped to reunite with them. Something big was happening and he was in the middle of it. Suddenly he felt like he had been caught up in a tornado and had no way of escaping.

"Simon?" Jacob's eyes fell on him. "You start."

Simon grinned. "I never expected we'd all end up in this area. We all had plans to go different ways. I didn't realize it was a home area for you, Jacob."

"I didn't either, but apparently it is. Mistletoe - who calls a town that?"

"Your great great grandfather apparently." Blackie grinned at him, then sobered. "We need to talk seriously, guys. Something is going on in Mistletoe and it revolves around both Finn and Whit."

"And I have no idea what it is. Finn doesn't either, I can tell you that. She thinks whatever has happened in the last couple of days goes back to an incident when she was a young teenager." A black look crossed his face. "She has told me she was attacked, beaten up, and threatened. She hasn't said who, but from what happened yesterday in her shop that I walked in on, I would said it was the chief's son who was the culprit." He brought the other two friends up to date on what had happened. He figured Blackie had told them what had gone on the night before.

The three other men exchanged glances. Finally, Simon spoke up. "But what brought you here, Whit?"

"My Grand left a letter and a journal for me, to be handed to me at his grave. I refused to read the letter, had no interest in coming this way. The lawyer finally tracked me down and specifically told me that Grand wanted me to come here, that his will would not be released or read until I had. So, you see? I had no choice." He paused, a thought crossing his mind. "I wonder how much he knew of what was going on here. I found Grams' journal in Finn's shop. She thought it came from a box of old books she had bought. But I wonder. Grand had gone on a trip about three weeks before he passed, when I was away overnight, or so his lawyer said. I wonder if he brought it here and stuck it in Finn's shop. He would have known I'd end up there. He knew my love of old books."

The three men with him stared at him for a moment before Josh spoke.

"You know, about that time an older gentleman came into the cafe, asked for tea and toast. He reminded me of someone and now I know it was you. I wonder if it was your grandfather. I meant to sit and talk with him but by the time it had settled down in there, he was gone.”

“It likely was him, Josh. He wouldn’t have mentioned it to me. Mistletoe had no meaning for me at that point. Now, I don’t know. Timothy tells me I own half the town buildings because Grand did.”

“Can your lawyer tell you if the police chief lives in one of your buildings?” Blackie was thinking ahead, knowing Jacob’s troubles were just starting.

Jacob stared at his mug, knowing he would need to ask, and dreading the answer. “I’ll ask him on Monday. He’s always unavailable on Sundays - he’s really involved in his church and has made that a day of rest his whole career.” He looked up, a bleak look on his face. “But where does that leave us with Finn?”

“With you, Jacob. She’s made a connection to you so quickly, I don’t know if I’ve seen anything like that before.” Simon studied his friend. “It has to be God, Jacob.”

Jacob stared at his friend. They had been through a lot together, those two friends, things not even their other two friends knew about. He finally nodded. "I think so, Simon. But how do I keep her safe?"

"Stick as close as you can. You'll be working through the journals, right? Can you do that at her shop?" Josh glanced at Blackie, seeing his nod.

"I can. She'll be able to tell me about the town and the people." He frowned, sitting back in his chair, and digging his hands into his pockets. He blew out a breath, searching the faces of his friends and then staring across the cafe. "I feel like I'm in over my head, guys."

"You are, Jacob. But you have us in your corner. No matter what happens, remember that God is in control." Simon stood. "Let's get you back to the hospital and see if we can sneak you in to see your lady."

Chapter 5

_L_eaning back in his chair, Jacob's eyes sought to find Finn among the shelving and displays in her store. When he couldn't see her, he rose, stretching, and then meandering slowly to the office. He propped himself against the office doorway, watching her deep in her work. A small sound roused her, and she looked up, blinking at him before she smiled. He winced as he saw the bruising on her face from the accident on the Saturday night.

"How are you feeling, Finn?"

She shrugged. "Like I was run over a truck." She stood, walking towards him. "How is your research coming?"

He shook his head. "I can't concentrate on it. The grief is too fresh for Grand, and I feel like I'm invading Grams' privacy looking at her journal."

"You're not, you know." She glanced back at her desk. "I'm caught up here for now. Let's take a look at them together." She reached out her hand, holding hers steady as he stared first at her and then her hand.

Jacob finally reached and grasped her hand. "Thank you, Finn. Having you here makes it easier. But first, let's pray. I know that whatever is in these books will change my life in a drastic manner and forever."

He sat once more at the desk she had told him to use and she scooted a chair close to him. He sighed as his phone chimed that he had a voice mail. He listened to it, a frown covering his face, before he tucked his phone away.

"That didn't sound like happy news." Finn watched him closely.

"No, it wasn't. I was asked the other night if the police chief lived in one of my buildings. It turns out he does. He tried to buy it years ago and every so often since. Grand refused to sell it to him." He paused, his eyes on her. "The lawyer didn't know why other than that Grand said he would never sell anything to that family."

She nodded. "I can see that. They have never been well liked in this town. We're still trying to figure out how he got to be chief. He had to have had something on someone to make it this far."

"More than likely he does. Simon is looking into that. His chief has asked him to. I turned over the video from the other night to them."

She sat back, before reaching for his grandmother's journal. "May I?"

He nodded. "Go ahead. I'll look through Grand's." He paused, fingering the letter from his grandfather he had never read.

"You need to read that first, Jacob."

He looked up at her, an expression on his face she couldn't read. He handed it to her. "Will you read it to me? It would be too hard reading it, seeing his handwriting. And knowing Grand, it will be written by hand."

She paused, staring down at the letter with just the word "Jacob" written on it. "Are you sure? This is likely pretty personal."

He gave a bark of laughter. "Nothing is so personal with that, I don't think, that I can't share with a treasured friend." He nodded. "Please."

She laid the letter down and rose. "I'm closing up the shop. We're going to go somewhere we can read it and look through the journals where I know we won't be disturbed. Grab your coat and your journals."

He hesitated for a moment, then did what she asked, his thoughts not on what he was doing, but on the lady walking away from him. Lord, I have no idea where this road is leading me, leading us. You are in control. I need to seek You in all things related to Grand's estate. I also need to seek Your will about Finn. I have never met anyone like her before.

Finn stood for a moment, watching him, not realizing her heart was in her eyes when he looked up. A smile creased his face as he reached for her hand.

"Come on, sweetheart. Show me where you want to go with these." He held up the journals.

She nodded. "We need to stop for one of our vehicles. I would say mine as I know where we need to go."

He shrugged. "Whatever. I've had females drive me before." He ducked as she swatted at him.

An hour later, Jacob stood on the porch of an old cabin, looking around, feeling the peace that came from the area. He saw the bits of snow that had accumulated under the trees where the sun couldn't reach.

"Who did you say owns this?" He turned as he heard Finn opening the door and then walking through, her footsteps echoing on the wooden floor.

"My Pops did. It's mine now. I think it goes back to his grandparents. I would imagine your grandfather was a frequent visitor here."

"I would think he would be." He stopped just inside the door, looking around. "This is nice, Finn. I like it. It's comfortable. It's like coming home."

She nodded, a grin on her face. "I'm so glad you feel like that. That's how I feel about it." She turned to head for the fireplace, when Jacob stopped her.

"Let me, okay?" Jacob crouched, reaching for the newspaper to crumble it and then layer the kindling and logs on it. He watched as the wood caught before he rose, finding Finn sitting on the couch watching him.

"Finn?"

"Why do I trust you, Jacob? I don't trust anyone else the way I trust you." She was genuinely puzzled.

He sat on the couch beside her, turning so he faced her. "I have no idea, Finn. Given what you've gone through in the last few days, I don't know who you'd trust in town, other than your family. And they can't be with you all the time."

She sighed, her head going back on the couch. "I know and they want to. But they smother me when they do that." She raised her head to stare at the fire. "You don't. You protect. You care. But you let me make the decisions I need to. You don't tell me what I have to do and demand I follow what you say."

Jacob shrugged. "You're your own person and have the right to make your decisions and to follow your heart. No one should ever force you to follow what they have determined you should follow. That's not how life works. That's not how God leads us."

She studied him for a moment before she nodded. "Whoever taught you that was very wise. You're a wise man, Jacob Whitson. I am honoured to be a friend of yours."

He grinned briefly. "Thank you, Finn. My grandparents raised me. My parents were overseas as missionaries and were killed in a typhoon when I was little. I had been left with Grand and Grams as Mom and Dad were only to be gone for three months. We didn't know they'd never come back."

"I'm sorry to hear that, Jacob." She paused. "Do you prefer Jacob or Whit, as your friends call you?"

"From you, Jacob." He reached for the letter he had set on the table near the couch. "I guess we can't put this off any longer, can we?"

She shook her head. "Do you still want me to read it? Or are you okay reading it?"

Jacob sat, the letter on his knee, his finger tracing his Grand's handwriting, struggling with the thought of reading his Grand's last letter to him. He blinked back the tears, praying for the strength and wisdom he suddenly knew he would need.

He finally looked up at Finn, handing her the letter. "I think you need to."

She nodded, her heart breaking for her friend. She prayed for him before she untucked the flap and pulled out the letter. Her eyes raised to his before he lowered his lashes, not willing to look at her. She sighed to herself. Lord, how do I do this? I need Your strength to help my friend.

She unfolded the letter, taking in the script of a scholarly man, turning to the end, seeing his signature. She raised her eyes once more to Jacob, who sat, hand covering his eyes. She swallowed hard and flipped back to the first page, finding it difficult to start

"Dear Jacob

"If you are reading this, then the Lord has called me home. I am ready to go, have been for many years, but I don't want to leave you alone, son.

"You never knew my history. I was very careful to keep it from you. Your father knew and we agreed that once you were a man, we would both talk to you. But God had other plans. Your father was called home as was your mother. When I went to talk to you, you were so excited about joining up with the armed forces, I didn't have the heart to talk with you then. I should have.

"You came home and I still couldn't talk to you. I should have, I know that now. I should have talked to you and prepared you for what I fear you are facing.

"You were directed to a small town called Mistletoe. You will find out its history over time but my family was one of the founding families. Over time, we have acquired many of the buildings and vacant land as people moved away, died, couldn't afford to live on the property any more. Anyone who sold us the land and still wanted to live there could, at no cost. That was one of the stipulations my father made. I pray that you will continue that. It's part of who we are as Christians to take care of those in need.

"Now, this is the hard part. I'm sending you back to a town where you'll find a family who has resented our family, the Adams, and a family named Bronagh, another one of the founding families. Another founding family, the Blackwells, left before my grandfather was born. I think your friend, Levi, is one of them. He is the image of a picture I have of one of the founders. There are two other founding families, whose names you'll discover over time.

"If you do go back, please be so careful. Don't trust everyone. If you have questions, call Norman Earl, my lawyer. He'll walk you through whatever it is you're facing. He's been back to Mistletoe for me many times. I was back just a few weeks ago. I needed to go, to leave something for you.

"If you go back, find Finn's. What I left for you is there. Finn, the young woman who owns the store now, is the image of her grandmother and from the little I spoke with her, has her character and love of people. She'll be your guide to what you need to find.

"Jacob, I love you, son. You have been a delight in our lives. You have become a man of God like few I have seen. Keep your hand to the plough that God has set before you. You will face dangers in the days ahead. That is something I regret I can't prevent. But know that you have friends and people who will stand with you. You are never alone.

"Love

"Grand."

Finn folded the letter, placing it carefully back into the envelope. She stood, her hand resting on Jacob's bowed head for a moment before she moved away, to the kitchen where she found a seat at the table, her head on her folded arms as tears flowed for her friend.

Chapter 6

$\mathcal{F}$inally raising his head, his hand on the letter, Jacob looked around, not seeing Finn. He had had no idea his grandfather would direct him to her. He thought he had chanced on her on his own. It must be God's hand, he thought. That's the only explanation. I could have gone anywhere, but Grand knew somehow I would end up in her store. Must be my love of old books.

He rose, looking for Finn, finding her sitting at the table in the little kitchen, a mug of tea in her hand. She looked up at him, her lashes still tear stained.

"Jacob?"

"Thank you, Finn. I couldn't have read it on my own." He dropped a kiss on the top of her head on his way by, not catching the stunned look on her face before she schooled her features.

"What will you do now?"

He sat in the chair beside her, his mug cradled in his hands, his face thoughtful. "I have no idea. At some point, I'll need to talk to Norman. He's our lawyer." He stared at his mug. "I have no idea who the family is." He looked up at her snort.

"You don't? You should."

"Tell me, Finn. Who do you think it is?"

"The Adams." Then, she paused. "No, that's too obvious. I have no idea then." She looked at him, fear momentarily crossing her face. "We need to find them and fast, Jacob. They won't want you to find out who they are."

He nodded. "I know, Finn. Grand named a family and I'll have to verify if it's them. And I fear that you're being my friend will bring trouble to you and your family." His face grew grave and new stern lines traced across it. "I don't want you or your family hurt. Maybe this wasn't such a good idea, coming here after all."

"I don't think you had much choice. You were meant to come here, Jacob. You may be the one who can break whatever hold this family has on our town." She sat back, her eyes on her friend. "There have always been undercurrents here, and no one has been able to pin down where the trouble started or who instigated it. Other than that caused by the Adams."

He sighed. "I know. I just don't like it that I brought danger to you." He searched her face, trying to get a sense of what she was thinking.

"You didn't, Jacob. Let me make that very clear. I may face something because of you, but I was already in danger. You walked in on it on Friday. But your grandfather was right. Let me repeat myself. There have always been undercurrents in town, that no one could define or get rid off. I think you're the one who will accomplish that. Fresh eyes and all."

Jacob shook his head. "I doubt that. It will take work and investigation." He rose and returned with the journals, setting them on the table in front of him. "It's getting late, Finn, and I need to get you back to town before it gets dark. I'm going to start with one of these. How be you take Grams' and read through it over the next few days? Make notes of anything that puzzles you. I'll do the same with Grand's. Then, we switch and read the other one. He brought Grams' here for a reason. I want to know why." He frowned as his phone chimed and he pulled it out. "Blackie. He's looking for us."

"Tell him we're on our way back. Twenty minutes should have us home. If we're not, tell him to find Peter and come looking for us at Pops' cabin."

Jacob nodded as he sent the message, then rose to put out the fire. He looked around the cabin, once more feeling the peace it gave him.

❀ ❀ ❀ ❀ ❀

Blackie watched Finn closely, noting the black circles under her eyes, the bruising on her forehead she tried hard to hide, the fatigue that dogged every move she was making and shook his head. She's just as stubborn as Whit, he decided. He rose from where he had been seated at their kitchen table and took the journal from her hands. Gently, he turned her towards the stairs to their upstairs, and hands on her shoulders, guided her to them.

She paused, not quite sure what was going on, but too tired to make a protest.

"Go to bed, Finn. Take a hot bath, a hot shower, soak for a bit. Then go to bed. You were in a serious accident two nights ago, spent that night in hospital, came home, went in to work today when you shouldn't have. You need rest. The journals can wait."

She shook her head. "But they can't, Blackie. They can't. Someone will be coming after Jacob, and the clue has to be in those books."

"Not tonight, Finn. Off to bed or I'll personally take you back to the hospital and have you admitted and placed under guard to keep you there."

She spun, mouth open at his words, staggering a little as the world around her spun. Blackie braced her up with a hand on her arm.

He smiled. "Go to bed, Finn. Jacob will still be here in the morning. I'm sending him to bed shortly too. I know he didn't sleep much on Saturday night, not worrying about you."

Jacob had watched their interaction from where he sat, not daring to rise and add his voice to what Blackie was saying. He watched in relief as she finally nodded and reached for the railing. Mary stood, stopping to hug Blackie, before she followed her daughter up the stairs.

Timothy watched in silence, waiting until the women had disappeared before he spoke.

"You've read the letter, Jacob?"

Jacob nodded, his eyes on the stairs where Finn had disappeared. "I did, Timothy. Grand mentioned Finn, that I should seek her out, that she would be of help to me." He looked at Timothy. "I don't want to involve her, Timothy. She'll get hurt."

Timothy shook his head, a small smile on his face. "It's too late, Jacob. You won't stop her now. She's like a terrier with a bone. She will not give up." He studied the younger man. "But that's not all, is it?"

Jacob shook his head, his eyes turning to Blackie. "Did your father ever speak of the other founding family?"

Blackie frowned, feeling the tension in Jacob and finding his eyes on him. He didn't understand.

Timothy swallowed the mouthful of tea he had just taken. "He used to talk of a family, but I can't recall the name off hand. It would be listed in the town hall. Why?"

"Because Grand mentioned the name. He told me I know someone who is the image of one of that family. That family moved from here years before Grand did."

Blackie's eyes darted between Timothy and Jacob, finally resting on Jacob. "Jacob?"

"It's your family, Blackie. The Blackwells. Grand said you were the image of one of them."

"Me? No way! We didn't come from here." He paused, trying to remember his family history. "At least, I don't think we did." He pulled out his phone. "I need to call my Mom. She'll know." He excused himself.

They watched him walk away. Then Timothy spoke. "Your grandfather was sure? Then we need to watch Blackie as well. Whoever it is seems to want to get rid of the founding families. They've gone after you two."

"How many families were there?" Jacob was still trying to absorb the fact that Blackie came from the same town his own roots did.

"Four, five, maybe. Finn would be able to find that out for you." Timothy sighed as he shifted in his chair. "We can't stop her, you know, Jacob. She will stay involved. Even if you tell her not to, she'll work away at it. And that will get her hurt."

"I know." Jacob ran his hands through his hair before clasping them together. "I want her to stay safe but I don't know how to."

"Stay with her, Jacob. She's made a connection to you like I have never seen before." He watched the emotions flickering across Jacob's face, emotions he didn't think Jacob had put a voice to yet. "Just watch her heart, Jacob. Don't hurt her that way."

Jacob's eyes shot to Timothy's, seeing the concern of a father in them. "I'll do my best not to. She's too precious to be hurt that way."

"She is. She's my little girl, always will be, even though she's an adult. Treat her as a precious jewel. That's all I ask." He rose, walking away from Jacob on those words.

Jacob watched him head for the stairs and sighed. He stood, pacing, knowing he needed sleep himself, but not willing to go. He reached for his grandfather's journal, but a hand on top of it stopped him from picking it up. He looked up, seeing Blackie's face.

"Blackie?"

Blackie nodded. "Your grandfather was right, Jacob. We were one of the founding families. I hate to tell you this but Mom went back through papers Dad has. We're not the only friends involved in this town."

Jacob sank into a chair. "Simon? Josh?"

Blackie nodded. "Both of them. They don't know it, I don't think. How did we all end up being friends and then back in this area?"

"God. It was His handiwork." Jacob sighed. "I want to read Grand's journal tonight, but I'm too tired."

"Go to bed, Whit. It will be there in the morning. I would suggest you lock them and the letter up somewhere safe."

Jacob nodded, fatigue suddenly setting in. "I will, Blackie. Good night." He dragged himself off to bed, not seeing Blackie watching him.

❀ ❀ ❀ ❀ ❀

Finn rose early the next morning, her body protesting every move she made. She sighed. She needed to be in the store, but today, she would have liked not to have been. She stood for a moment on the porch, eying the steps before she walked down and towards the downtown area. She hadn't seen Jacob yet and hoped he wouldn't show up too soon. She sighed as she reached her shop.

Jacob sat on the bench outside the door, reading.

Jacob looked up as he heard footsteps stop in front of him and grinned. "Finn! Fancy meeting you here."

"Jacob. You need your rest."

He stood, looking down at her upturned face. "Not as much as you. Here. Let me unlock the door for you."

She refused to give up the key, giving him a grumpy look before she stopped and then turned to apologize.

"It's okay, Finn. Really. I shouldn't be taking up your time." Jacob moved to walk away when her hand on his arm stopped him. He stood, his back to her, a rejected feeling in his heart.

"No. You do need to be here. Let me get through what I need to first, and then I'll work on the journal."

He nodded even as she turned away. Something had changed, he thought, and I'm not sure what or how. He prayed for his friend, then lifted his eyes to search the surrounding area. He could feel someone watching them, someone close, but he couldn't see anyone. He did not like that feeling at all.

He was soon immersed in his grandfather's journal, jotting notes and names down. He finally sat back, glancing at his watch. It was lunchtime and he knew Finn had not stopped all morning.

Chapter 7

$\mathcal{F}$inn looked up as she felt watched, her eyes on the doorway. No one stood there. She rose, searching the building, not seeing anyone, not even Jacob. She hesitated beside the desk he had been using, seeing his notes and the journal, but not him. She shivered, her hands rubbing up and down her arms. Something was off in the building and she didn't know what.

She turned as she heard the doorbell and tilted her head to watch the two men walking towards her. One was Blackie. She didn't know the other man. She walked behind the counter, her hands shoved into her sweater pocket, clenched into fists. She felt that this visit was going to change everything.

"Finn? How are you today?" Blackie stopped in front of the counter, head tilted to study her.

She shrugged. "I don't know. How am I supposed to feel?" She shook her head. "I'm sorry. I shouldn't take it out on you.

83

I'm never grumpy and this is the second time I've had to apologize this morning."

Blackie grinned at her. "Not a problem. You've been through a lot. You're entitled to feel beaten up and worn down." He glanced as the man standing beside him. "Finn, this is another of our friends. Simon Gardner. He's a lieutenant with the county force."

She held up a hand to stop him, her eyes on Simon. "The county force? What is it with you four? You meet in the armed forces, go your separate ways, and all end up here."

Simon started to laugh at her, his eyes sparkling at her question and in response to the glint of mischief he saw in her eyes, even as he turned to face the door as it opened, Jacob walking through with bags of takeout food.

"Harassing a store owner, guys? That's not like you." He grinned at his friends as he set the food down on the counter. "Josh said you two were heading this way and sent your favourites." He paused as he peeked into the bags. "At least, what he sent used to be your favourites."

Blackie shook his head at him before he turned to Finn. "Where can we sit and eat, Finn? Jacob called in reinforcements to look at some of the journal entries, but we need to eat first. Growing boys and all, you know."

Finn laughed at his nonsense before pointing towards the desk Jacob had been using that morning. "There, I think. You three have a seat. I have a call coming in that I need to take and then I'll join you."

The three men watched her walk away, Jacob's eyes lingering on her, not seeing the looks his friends were exchanging. Yes, they both thought as they nodded. Jacob's found his lady, whether he realizes it or not. Protect them, Lord, was their prayer.

Simon wiped his mouth on his napkin, his eyes on Finn. She was uncomfortable, he could tell, and kept glancing around the store. He rose, asking Finn to show him something on the other side of the store.

"Finn? You're nervous and keep looking around. Why?" Simon's keen eyes assessed her as she hesitated to respond.

She shuddered once more as she looked around. "I feel like I am being watched, but that's ridiculous. It's just the four of us here. How could I have that feeling?"

"Have you had it before?"

She nodded. "Just before you and Blackie walked in. I don't like it, Simon."

He gave a sigh. "Then there's something here making you nervous. Let me look around. If I don't find anything with a quick look, I'll come back after you close and we'll search. If you have that feeling, then you're not wrong. With what you've been going through, I could see someone sticking in a camera or something." He looked at Jacob standing just behind Finn. "Go with Whit, Finn. Work on those journals. That's where the answer likely lies."

She nodded, turning to walk away and walked right into Jacob, whose arms came around her to steady her. She hesitated, then hugged him, before moving past him to her office. She needed a few minutes to compose herself. Being around Jacob was disturbing her, but in a good way. She needed to try and sort out her thoughts, but couldn't. Lord, please help me. I'm in over my head right now. It's not enough that I have to deal with Adams and their threat. Now you send someone like Jacob into my life. Him and his friends.

Jacob watched her walk away before he turned to Simon. "What was that all about?"

"She's feeling watched. She felt it this morning when you were out getting our lunch." Simon turned in a circle, assessing the store. "There are many places someone could hide a camera."

"And we need to find them, if they're really here." He looked around. "I'd start with her security cameras. There are four of them. Someone could hack into them." He pointed them out. "I'll have her call the company and see what they can find out." He walked away, heading to find his lady.

Blackie watched from where he sat, a finger holding his place in Grams' journal. He had come across something he needed to talk to Jacob about, but it didn't look as it would happen then. He marked the place, and pulled out his phone as it rang. Not now, he thought. I don't need any distractions.

Simon finally turned back to where Finn stood watching him, seated behind her counter, paperwork spread out in front of her. He could see the apprehension on her face. He looked down at the electronics he had found. Someone had definitely wanted to keep her under surveillance, but what they had installed was overkill, he thought.

Finn watched as he sorted out the cameras and microphones, sticking each one into an evidence bag and then labelling them before he pulled off his latex gloves. "Don't you have to turn them into the police here? If you do, I can guarantee they'll disappear."

Simon shook his head. He had already talked to his supervisor. "No. This is not a crime scene. You asked a friend for help. Just because your friend is a police officer doesn't matter. I'll take them to our own lab and have them run them."

Finn had been searching his face. "You're not expecting to find out anything, are you?"

He shook his head, his eyes finding Jacob's. "Not likely. But I do know these are not an average run-of-the-mill pieces of equipment. They were likely found on the black market."

Jacob's hand rested on the back of Finn's chair as he leaned in to take a look at them. "They're very sophisticated, aren't they? Somehow, I don't think Adams would have the knowledge of where to find them."

Simon nodded, his stance tense as a thought crossed his mind before he shrugged it off. There was no way, he thought, that man would be here in Mistletoe, not this far out of the way. "I'll see what the lab says. Now, about your journals. Find anything interesting?"

Jacob nodded as he placed Grand's journal down on the counter. "Bits and pieces that I'll have to work through. He gives a lot of names that I'll have to research." He turned as Blackie stopped beside him. "Blackie?"

"I found an interesting reference a couple of years before your Grams died, Jacob. She mentions a man who came looking for your grandfather. She didn't know him, and he wouldn't leave a name. But she did give a description of him." He found the page and read it aloud, stopping as he heard a sound from Finn. "Finn?"

She looked at him in horror before turning to Jacob, her hand on his arm. "That's Chief Adams. How did he find your grandparents?"

"Easy. He could use his resources to do so. But why? Grams didn't say." He looked down at his Grand's journal. "I didn't see anything where Grand mentions that visit, but he does talk about Adams early on. I think he was one of the reasons Grand walked away from this town." He raised his eyes to Simon. "What can we find out about Adams and his past?"

"I can do some digging, but there's a lot buried in this town that people aren't going to talk about. It will take a lot of work, Jacob, and I'm not sure we'll have the time we'll need to do that."

Blackie spoke up. "Let Josh and I work on it, okay? This is right up the line of work I'm taking up."

Jacob leaned against the counter, his eyes thoughtful as he watched his friend. "You have never said what line of work you've gone into."

Blackie shook his head. "No, I haven't. It's no secret. I've taken up investigations, mainly concentrating of past histories of people. That's what Dad does and he's trained me. I can pretty much work from anywhere."

"I had forgotten that, Blackie. That's wonderful. I'm not sure how you ended up here but I'm glad the three of you are." Jacob looked up at the clock. "Time to close up, my love. Your Mom will be waiting for you."

His two friends exchanged glances even as they moved towards the door, Blackie shaking his head at Simon. They realized Jacob's endearment for Finn had slipped out.

Jacob finally laid his Grand's journal down and rising from the armchair in his room, stretched, his glance going to the clock. It was late night or rather early morning. He needed to talk to Norman that day, to find out what he knew. He didn't want to make the drive the four hundred miles away and leave Finn on her own. He feared for what might happen to her. He still hadn't acknowledged what was growing in his heart, thinking it too soon.

He sat on the edge of his bed, the low light leaving most of the room in darkness. His thoughts drifted to what Simon had found that day in Finn's store and he frowned. He didn't think the police would have done that. But who then?

He finally gave up and laid down, pulling the quilt over him. He didn't think he would sleep but he did. He didn't look out the window, didn't see the figure standing there watching the house, his eyes on Jacob's room and then seeking Finn's. An angry growl came from the person before steps led them away.

Chapter 8

Jacob slowly laid his phone down on the desk and stared at his notes. Talking to his lawyer, Norman, had given him information that he had not expected. His grandfather had been researching the people in the town and left quite a packet of information with Norman, who indicated he would drive over with it. He told Jacob that once he was in the town, Aaron had not wanted Jacob to leave it, not until he had resolved whatever the underlying issues were. Norman could explain no more than that.

He felt a hand laid gently on his shoulder, and looking up, saw Finn standing beside him, a softened look on her face, a mug of tea being set down beside him. He reached up to clasp her hand but before either of them could speak, a customer called for assistance. He heard Finn sigh as she walked away, still limping slightly from the bruising she had taken from the car accident. He reached for his mug, sipping absentmindedly as his mind once more went to his notes. He knew Finn had his Grams' journal and that it was time he looked at it. He tidied up his papers, slipping them into his briefcase before he picked it up and headed for her office.

Finn's eyes followed Jacob as he walked towards the office before she returned her attention to her customers. Business was picking up as it always did at this time of year, with all the tourists coming in just to say they had spent December in Mistletoe. An underlying sense of danger permeated the air around her and she didn't like it one bit.

She turned back as a question was asked regarding some old tools and her mind once more focused on her work. She would talk to Jacob later.

Finally, the end of the day came and with a sigh of relief and fatigue, she locked the door, turning off lights as she walked back towards the office. She stood in the doorway, finally leaning against the doorjamb as she watched Jacob deep at work, his hair ruffled from running his hands through it, the shadow of a beard on his face, and knew that she hoped he never left that town, never left her.

Jacob heard a faint sound and looked up, his face lighting up as he saw Finn, and then the darkened store behind her.

"It's that time of day already?" He stood, gathering his work and stuffing it into his briefcase.

"It is. I'm all locked up. We can go out the back and set the alarm there." She waited for him to follow her, holding the door as he left and punching in the code before shutting the door and locking it. "Did you have a successful day?"

He nodded. "I did. Norman's heading this way in the next couple of days. Grand had a bunch of material for me, that Norman was only to give me if I asked for it." He sighed. "I have no idea why Grand did it this way."

"Likely he wasn't sure you would come here. He also didn't want to influence you at first."

Jacob reached for her hand, drawing her close to him. "I think you may be right. If Norman hadn't pushed me, I not likely would have come. And I would have missed meeting you."

She tilted her head to study him, and then nodded. "I would not have liked not to have met you." She laughed at herself. "Does that even make sense?"

He laughed as he followed her up the steps to the B&B. "It does, somehow. Let's compare notes after supper, if you're up to it. You're still hurting, my love, and I don't like that."

She stopped walking and turned to face him, hearing the endearment once more from him. Her mouth opened to question him, then snapped shut.

Mary turned as they entered the kitchen, Jacob setting his briefcase down out of the way.

"Did Blackie find you, Jacob? He was looking for you about an hour ago."

He shook his head. "No. And I didn't get a message from him. He'll catch up with me tonight if not before. What can I do to help?"

Mary stood for a moment, her eyes taking in the young man standing in front of her, an engaging grin on his face. "I need the table set. Put on a place for Blackie. I think he said he'd be back for supper."

"I can do that." Jacob headed to the small powder room to wash up, leaving the two woman staring after him and then at one another.

"Is he for real?" Finn's low voice caught her mother's ear.

Mary smiled. "He is, Finn. That he is. I pray he never leaves this house."

Finn stared at her mother, her mouth open before she snapped it closed. No way, she thought. He'll find someone somewhere and be off.

Blackie stood for a moment, assessing Jacob. He could see the stress in his friend, knowing how much this was weighing on him. He prayed for him, even as he wondered at Jacob's grandfather putting him through this. But then, again, he thought, he never got a chance to talk to him, or didn't take a chance he should have. He slid into a chair near Jacob, causing him to look up.

Jacob's eyes narrowed as he looked at his friend. Something was up, he thought. His eyes moved to Finn, who was curled up in an easy chair, a book open on her lap, but she was staring into the open flame in the fireplace.

"Blackie?" Jacob's voice was low as he spoke.

"Jacob. We need to talk, somewhere Finn isn't around. Come up to my room. No, that won't work." Blackie was frustrated.

"How about going to see Josh? Would that work? Somehow I think what you're about to say involves him too. Besides, I need to talk to you two and Simon about something I found in the journal."

Blackie nodded as he rose and headed for the front door, grabbing his jacket and boots as he did so. Jacob hesitated for a moment, but didn't want to disturb Finn so he walked quietly away.

Josh stood for a moment, staring at the two men standing there, and then at Simon walking towards them. "Come on in. I can see I'm not going to have a peaceful evening."

Jacob nodded. "I'm sorry, Josh. I don't think you will. Not with what I think Blackie has to say or what I have to say."

Settling down around Josh's living room with their mugs of coffee or tea, the four men looked at one another before Simon spoke.

"I can tell this isn't just a social call. How be we spend some time in prayer first?"

Jacob finally looked at Blackie. "What was it you wanted to talk to me about?"

Blackie stared at him. "I know your family was one of the founding ones. I have information as to why your grandfather left. I don't think it's common knowledge or that he would have put it into his journals. I'm guessing you knew his parents died early, in a fire, but not that the fire was deliberately set. Your grandfather wasn't home that night. He had gone to stay with Timothy and his family at their cabin. No one ever told Aaron that they suspected murder." Blackie watched with compassion as Jacob absorbed that. "I'm tracking back through who would have wanted him dead. I'm not getting far, but I do have a couple of names to give to Simon."

"That explains a lot." Jacob was thoughtful. "Grand was always so careful of fire and hazards like that. He never said and I thought it was just him being him."

Simon spoke up. "I can track the name but it may not do any good after all that time."

"It won't but if we can find out who, then we can deal with them." Blackie pulled a paper from his pocket and handed it over to Simon. "These are just some of them. There's someone in the background I haven't been able to identify just yet."

Jacob leaned over to read the names, before nodding. "I've met some of the family. They acted scared when they hear my name. That would be why." He leaned back in his chair, his eyes searching the faces of his friends. "Now, for my news. It's really earthshaking when you think of it. How long have we been friends? And we came from different areas of the country.

"I did some research and my grandfather's letter has confirmed the facts as has my lawyer, Norman. All of our families were founding families here in Mistletoe." He sat back, seeing the stunned locks on the other three men's faces.

"How can that be? No one ever said anything." Josh was puzzled. "And how did we all end up here anyway?"

"I have no idea, Josh, and it was God. It had to be Him leading us all here."

Blackie spoke up. "So, now that we're here, what's the purpose?"

Jacob shrugged. "I have no idea. But I think there is someone hidden here that needs to be removed, and we're the ones who will do it. We're outsiders, even though we have history here and can see things others can't. Let me explain further about the journals and what Norman had to tell me."

Four hours later, Blackie and Jacob headed for the B&B, their words quiet in the night air. Despite discussing the situation for hours, none of them had come closer to a solution or a name.

Jacob walked through the downtown area the next morning, his eyes assessing the buildings. He wasn't sure which ones he owned but he did want to know. He could see most were in good shape, well painted but a few had begun to become rundown. *Don't let those ones be mine. And if they're not, let me be able to buy them.* He turned as he heard his name called and reached to shake Norman's hand.

"Norman. You made good time."

Norman, a man in his late-twenties, grinned. "It helps to have a cousin with their own airplane. We flew into the large city about an hour from here and then rented a car. John came with me. He wanted to see this town and say he was in Mistletoe in December." Norman looked around. "This is something. I've been here in the spring and summer but never this close to winter."

"It is something. It's peaceful and really stirs those memories of being a kid. But there is an undercurrent here, one I'm picking up on."

Norman nodded. "I know there is. Now, where can we talk?"

"How be we head back to the B&B? I left all my information there this morning."

Four hours later, Jacob sat back in his chair, his mind whirling. "That much information Grand had found? How?"

Norman shrugged. "I guess because he knew the families and knew what to ask for. He hired a private investigator to come in and search through records." He paused. "Now, what was the name of that investigator?"

"Blackwell?"

Norman's eyes shot to him. "It was. How did you know?"

"Because his son is a good friend of mine and is in town now. Levi Blackwell."

Norman nodded and then stood. "I'll leave this with you, then. You and your friends need to be very careful. Whoever this is will stop at nothing. You've already seen some of the steps he'll take."

"But the attacks were directed at Finn."

"The first one from that Adams character was directed at her. I think you'll find any additional ones and those cameras and listening devices Simon found are directed at you. You spend a lot of time in her shop. They have to be able to track you somehow and that's one way they can."

Jacob slowly sank back into his chair. "You mean, I'm bringing danger to this family?"

Norman gave a small smile. "We have no idea if that's true or not, but you do need to take precautions. You and your friends and Finn and her family."

He walked away, leaving Jacob sitting there, a stunned look on his face. He didn't hear Finn enter, didn't see her hesitate before she approached him, her hand rubbing against his back before she sat in a chair near him.

He looked up finally, seeing her sitting there, a frown on her face.

"Jacob? Did Norman come today?"

Jacob nodded. "He did. We spent the last four hours going over everything." He sat back, his eyes dropping to the pile of paperwork on the table in front of him. "It's not good, Finn. We can't figure out who is behind it all. And he said you and your family are in danger. But we don't know who all from, other than Adams. And they have gone into hiding."

Finn shook her head at him. "Your head's spinning right now, I imagine. Set it aside for overnight. I want you to come to our prayer meeting tonight. It will do you good."

He nodded, his eyes finally leaving the paperwork in front of him. "I have something else you need to know, and I'm not sure how to tell you."

Her heart sank. Did he already have a lady friend? "What is it, Jacob?"

"It's like this. Blackie, Josh, Simon and I met years ago. We came from different areas of the country, from the four corners of it I guess you could say. The thing of it is, all our families have roots here. All of them were one of the founding five families."

Finn sat back, not quite sure whether to believe him or not. "And none of you knew?" When he shook his head, she rose and began to pace. "Then, they'll be at risk as well, won't they? Whoever this is won't stop until he has chased you four away or killed you. What secret is he or she hiding?"

"That's interesting. You don't automatically assume it's a man."

She spun, fire flying from her eyes. "Why would I? Women can be just as dangerous as men and more so as they are not expected to do something like this." She reached for his hand, pulling him to his feet. "Come. Mom left dinner ready for us. We just have to heat it. She was over in the county seat today and thought she might be late getting back."

Mary stood for a moment, watching the two work together to put the meal on the table. She sighed, knowing that her daughter's heart had already been caught by Jacob but not sure how he felt. Then, she paused as she caught him looking at Finn without Finn seeing him, his heart on his face and in his eyes, that he quickly schooled away. Lord, don't let either of them hurt the other. They're so good together, bringing out the best in one another. I can see that already. Protect and hide their hearts until Your timing is right.

"Mom! I didn't hear you come in." Finn moved to hug her mother. "Jacob's coming to prayer meeting tonight."

"He is, is he? Then you'd better get a move on. It starts in an hour and we still have to eat. Dad and Peter will eat after, Dad said."

"Oh, okay. I thought they'd be here." Finn moved to remove their place settings

even as Jacob slid the lasagna pan onto the
hot plate on the table, then waited to seat the
ladies before he seated himself, not thinking
anything of it.

Chapter 9

Finn paced her store, not quite sure what the problem was. It was busy enough, she thought, I need to look at hiring someone, even just to run the cash, and train them to work the store. The online store is so busy, it would take up all my time if I let it.

She turned as she heard an unwanted voice behind her. Gerry Adams stood there.

"You need to leave, Gerry. You're not welcome in this store."

"And you'll leave with me. I checked. Your boyfriend's not in here today."

"But there are plenty of other customers. You won't want me to start screaming, now would you?" Finn looked behind him and saw Josh approaching, a relieved feeling coursing through her. "Josh. Just the person I needed to see. And Simon. He's with you."

Simon stood for a moment, assessing the man in front of him, before removing his handcuffs and approaching Gerry. "He's bothering you again, is he, Finn? That's okay. I can remove him for you. We need to talk to him over at County. It seems as if he's been up to no good over there."

Gerry turned, staring Simon up and down. "You're not taking me anywhere. You have no idea who I am." His voice was loud enough to attract the attention of the customers, who gathered around, peering at the activity and whispering among themselves.

"Yes, actually, I do. Your father can't help you out on this one. What you did wasn't here in Mistletoe." He snapped the cuffs around Gerry's wrists. "I have a car outside just waiting for you. And don't think your friends will help. They won't want to get involved. Finn, I don't think he'll be back for a while. At least I pray he won't be."

"Thank you, Simon." Josh stood at her shoulder as she watched the two men walk from the store and Gerry be stuffed into the back seat of Simon's cruiser.

"Take some time, Finn. I'll run your cash for you. It can't be that different from mine."

"Thank you, Josh. Bless you. Give everyone here a 10% discount for their trouble." She moved away, quiet words of thanks coming to her, words of support coming from the townsfolk.

Jacob walked into the store, staring at Josh behind the counter, before he shot a look behind him.

"Josh? Who's running the cafe?"

Josh looked up, a grin on his face. "Faith is. I came here to speak to Finn with Simon and we found Gerry Adams here. Simon arrested him and carted him off to County."

"Oh, I see. He won't be back?"

Josh shook his head. "Not for a few days and longer if Simon and his chief have their way." He nodded to the office. "Finn's back there. I offered to help for now."

"Thank you, Josh." Jacob headed for the office, stopping back from the door to watch Finn.

Finn had become immersed in her online sales and had almost forgotten that she had a store to run. She knew she was in denial, that she really didn't think Gerry would have appeared as he had, but he did and was now out of the town. For good, she prayed. She looked up at a small sound, fright momentarily crossing her face until she saw Jacob standing there, moving towards her as she looked up, to catch her close in a hug.

"You're okay?" Jacob stood back, his hands on her arms.

"I am, thanks to Josh and Simon. What was he thinking?" She could feel the rage rising within her once more.

Jacob grinned at her and then grabbed her hand, pulling her through the store to the back door. "Come out here for a moment."

"I don't have a jacket, Jacob. I'll freeze."

"It's not that cold today. You won't freeze."

He turned to face here as she stood, back to the door, watching him intently. "I'm glad you're okay. And that Simon and Josh were here. Who knows what he would have done."

She nodded, not able to speak.

"I spent the morning going through town. Then I talked to Norman. There are some buildings that are getting run down. I don't own them but if God is willing, I will and I can renew them. Norman talked to the owners. They should be making a living but they're paying someone for protection."

"Protection? A protection racket in this town? But who?" Finn was shocked.

"I have a good idea who and Blackie is working on that with his Dad. By the way, did I tell you we're all founding family members?"

She looked at him, not quite sure if he had or not. "I didn't know that. Wow! Life is strange, isn't it? So now what happens? Do you all just leave again?"

"I'm not leaving here, Finn. Not until I die. I like it here. And there is someone here to keep me here." He watched her face intently, seeing when she comprehended what he had to say and paled at his words. "Come on. Let's get you back inside. Josh needs to get back to his cafe."

"Josh! I forgot all about him!" Finn yanked the door open, running into the store, intent on finding Josh and apologizing.

Jacob roused in the night, hearing a sound from outside. He rose, pulling on his clothes and reaching for his jacket. He crept down the stairs, pulling on his boots and then opening the door as silently as he could. He crouched down, his eyes searching the backyard, finally seeing a figure hiding in the trees. Breathing a prayer of thanks that it was a cloudy night, he moved through the yard towards the figure, not seeing the man rising up behind him until he heard a whisper of a sound. Turning too late, he crumpled to the ground, eyes closed, blood already streaming from the blow to the back of his head.

The man from the back of the yard approached, his booted foot reaching to shove Jacob over onto his back. The two men stood arguing before one of them stooped, pulling Jacob to his feet and draping him over his shoulder. They made their way to the waiting truck, dumping Jacob into the bed of it before they climbed into the cab, pulling away as silently as they could.

Timothy touched the door the next morning, a frown in place. He knew it had been locked the night before, he had checked it himself. He glanced at the boots sitting by the door and realized Jacob's were missing. He turned, heading for Blackie's room to rouse him. Jacob was missing, he was sure.

Blackie stared at Timothy, then turned to reach for his clothes. "What time do you think, Timothy?" His voice was low.

"It must have been early. It's only five a.m. now."

Blackie nodded as he followed Timothy out the back door, shrugging on his jacket. "We need to call the police."

Timothy snorted. "It won't do any good."

"Then we tell them it's Aaron Whitson's grandson."

"No, that's not our place. Tom will help. Let me go call him." Timothy headed back for the house even as Blackie pulled out his phone.

"Simon. Sorry to wake you so early. Whit's missing. Yeah, sometime earlier this morning. Timothy found the back door unlocked when he came down to the kitchen." Blackie walked through the yard, stopping near a disturbed patch of snow and looking back towards the house and then towards the back of the yard. "From what I'm seeing, he came out, was ambushed, and then carted away. No, we won't disturb anything. Timothy went to call Tom, an officer here he can trust. Oh. Okay. I'll tell him." Blackie pocketed his phone as Timothy approached.

"Tom's on his way. He won't bring anyone else in until he sees what's up."

"Simon's on his way. He's bringing one of their lab techs with him. He says the county force will be moving in today to take over leadership of this force. That won't go over well."

"It will go over better than he expects. People have be running scared for months and years now of Adams and his cronies. If they clean up the force, then I welcome their involvement."

Blackie nodded as he searched the area with his eyes, desperately seeking his friend. "He said his chief talked to the town council and mayor and was asked to step in, now that Adams is hiding. And Simon arrested Gerry Adams yesterday in Finn's shop." He stopped at a sound from Timothy. "You didn't know he came back around?"

Timothy shook his head, even as he heard a voice behind him.

"Dad? What are you two doing out here at this time of the morning?" Finn stood watching them.

The two men shared a look before Timothy moved to his daughter, an arm coming around her to lead her back to the house. "I've got some back news, love. Jacob must have heard something or came out here for some reason. We can't find him."

Finn's feet stopped moving abruptly and she spun to look behind her, causing her father's arm to drop away from her. "Jacob? Missing? Oh, no! Who?"

"That's what we'll find out. Tom's coming from our force. Simon's on his way over as well. I have news that you'll like. County is taking over our force for now."

"Well, that's something. It's about time. But it doesn't solve the mystery of where Jacob is, or why, or who?"

"No, it doesn't. But we need you to stay inside. I'll arrange for someone to be with you at your shop. If they've taken Jacob from here, who knows where they'll take you from."

"But I don't think I'm a target, Dad." Finn was digging in her heels, not willing to admit that she might be.

"It doesn't matter. If Jacob gets away or they want to play with his mind, they'll take you to get to him. You've been seen together in town. You're never with a male friend, only with your brother or me. That will tell whoever is watching you two he means something to you." His facial expressions softened. "I don't know what he means to you now or in the future. But we need to keep you safe. He would want that."

She agreed, feeling grumpy and disgruntled that she had to be watched. Then she sighed. Lord, improve my attitude. I need to stay safe, I get that, but I can't stop living my life. I have a store to run and need to be there. I have a life to live. Protect Jacob, please, Dear Lord. Bring him back to us safely.

Four hours later, Simon pushed open the door to Finn's store and stepped inside, pausing to watch as she worked with a customer. Her head raised as she saw him and then nodding went back to her customer. Simon wandered through the store, searching for evidence of tampering and finding none. He had talked to her security company and they couldn't see where her system had been hacked at all.

"Simon. Have you news?" Finn's voice was quiet behind him.

Simon turned. "Not yet, but we're working on it. We'll find him for you, Finn.

Trust us on that." He looked around, seeing no one else in the store. "I need to talk to you about your own safety."

She scowled at him. "I don't need a protector."

He held up a finger, stopping her words. "That's not a decision you can make. It's already been made for you. I'm here for the rest of the day. Starting tomorrow, we have one of our officers who will come in and work with you on a daily basis. We have another one that will take a room in the B&B. That is for your family's sake as well as yours. Your parents have agreed to it."

She scowled at him again and then shrugged. "Then I guess I have help tomorrow. I can close up now, it's close enough." She turned to walk away, stopping to say over her shoulder, "And I suppose you're walking me home."

He grinned at her back. "Actually, driving you home. No walking on your own for the foreseeable future."

Finn's head dropped for a moment, then Simon watched as her shoulders tightened. "I guess that's that then, isn't it?"

Chapter 10

$\mathcal{R}$eaching for the back of his head and the pain he could feel, Jacob roused slowly, his body rocking back and forth with the movement of the truck. He shivered, not quite comprehending why he was so cold. He raised his head, his eyes blinking in the near dawn light as they slowly focused on where he was. He groaned as he remembered walking out into the yard and then nothing. He raised his head enough to look towards the front of the truck, knowing he would have to escape somehow and not quite sure how he would. The truck slowed as the driver negotiated a turn, and Jacob took advantage of that, reaching for the side and pulling himself up and over, rolling away from the narrow dirt track the truck was on. He rolled until he came under a tree and stopped, his head on his arms, trying to catch his breath.

He struggled to his feet, knowing he had to get away, but not knowing where he was or where he should go. He stumbled as he blindly walked forward. He had no idea how far from Mistletoe he even was. He had no idea of how long he had been unconscious. He paused, his eyes struggling to focus on his watch. It had been an hour. They could have taken him anywhere in that time.

He paused, his head turned to listen for his kidnappers but he heard nothing. He knew they would be back, would be trying to track him. Stumbling forward, he moved his feet, his head pounding with each step.

Finally, he had to stop. He sank down, his back against a fallen tree, his knees raised as he folded his arms on them and rested his head down. He didn't think he could take another step. His vision faded as he lost the battle to stay awake and alert.

He had no idea how long it was before he felt hands on his arms, on his head bandaging his wound. He didn't hear the call for help or see the officials that ran towards him. He didn't feel himself lifted to a stretcher and then carried back to the nearby road and lifted into an ambulance, that raced away to take him to safety, a police officer in the back with him.

Simon stood with the young couple who had found him, a young couple out looking for a Christmas tree. He took their statement and then turned as he heard the barking of the K-9 unit that had responded.

He sighed. He wanted to go with Jacob but he was needed here. He looked around the area, not expecting to find anything, and he was right. So close to town, yet not so close. He thought through the distance. The kidnappers must have driven around for a while. They really weren't that far from the B&B.

Finn looked up as she heard the door to her shop open and saw her father walking towards her, a grim look on his face. She stepped backwards, her head shaking from side to side, even as the female officer braced her arm behind her.

"Dad? Please! Don't tell me!" Tears choked her voice.

"He's found, Finn. Simon called about ten minutes ago. They found him and are on the way to the hospital with him. Let Candy close up for you. Leave your keys and your code. She'll open for you in the morning as well." He looked past Finn at Candy, who nodded.

"I can do that, Mr. Bronagh. I have no problem with that. Finn's so thorough with her research and description of the articles, I don't think I'll have any problems tomorrow. I can always call her if I need to."

Finn turned to hug Candy before she ran for her jacket, shoving her arms in the sleeves as she ran back, her purse slipping down from her shoulder. Timothy stopped her, straightened her jacket and zipped it closed, then pushed her purse strap back on her shoulder before drawing her into a hug. He tucked her into the car and headed for the nearby county town.

Timothy pulled into the hospital parking lot and reached for his daughter's arm, startling her into looking at him.

"Before we go in, Finn, we need to pray for him. Simon said he was unconscious from a head wound. He didn't know how far Jacob had struggled to walk when I talked to him but he thought miles. Just remember that we really don't have any right to see him." She frowned at him when he said that. "We're not family. We may need to contact his lawyer to get permission to see him."

Finn shook her head. "I'll get in, Dad. Trust me. They won't keep me out." She was out of the car and running for the doors before her father could respond.

Timothy searched for Finn when he entered, his eyes not seeing her but seeing Josh and Blackie waiting for him.

"Where is she?"

"She headed back. I have no idea what she said to the clerk but they let her in." Blackie turned to study the doors to the exam rooms. "You don't think she said she was his girlfriend, do you?"

Timothy groaned. "That's exactly what she would do. I need to have a talk with her." He moved to walk towards the clerk, but Josh's hand on his arm stopped him.

"Let her go, Timothy. I think that's how Jacob thinks of her. It's there when he looks at her. If it's okay with you, she'll need to be there and he'll need her."

Timothy nodded. "I know. But she shouldn't be stretching the truth like that."

"No, she shouldn't. Talk with her later. Right now, we need her with Jacob. He has no one else."

Finn regretted running from her father, and she didn't like that she hadn't told the whole truth to the clerk. She wasn't officially Jacob's lady but he made her feel like he wanted her to be. The nurse looked around as she paused in the doorway before she smiled and beckoned her forward.

"Are you family?" The words were quiet.

"No, a good friend. He has no living family. Not any more." Finn's eyes pleaded for understanding and the nurse nodded.

"That's fine. If you're a good friend, then we'll let you stay. Let me have your name and I'll add it to his record." She turned to study Jacob. "He's not from here, is he? He looks familiar."

Finn took another look at the nurse. "Caitlin? Is that you?"

Caitlin turned. "Finola. I didn't recognize you for a moment. It's been a long time. How do you know this man?"

"He turned up about a week ago in Mistletoe and is staying with Mom and Dad. His grandfather was Aaron Whitson."

"Whitson? Oh my! What a greeting to give to a Whitson! Of course, we'll let you stay."

"How is he?" Finn moved forward, her hands gripping the bed rail as she watched Jacob's head twist and turn.

"The doctor's been in and out. We'll be sending him for some imaging to make sure there is no damage other than a concussion. He'll be staying for a day or so. But if he's with your people, then I know he'll be discharged sooner."

Finn nodded, before she turned. "We have a friend of his staying at the B&B as well. Blackie was a medic in the army, so he'll keep an eye on him."

"Well, I must say, you're well prepared for this."

Finn gave a small smile. "God knew what we needed and prepared it all."

Caitlin's smile faltered. She didn't share Finn's confidence in God, not any more. She wished she did. She had become cynical over time and regretted that.

Finn stepped aside as they came for Jacob, moving back towards the waiting room, just hesitating to get a promise from Caitlin to come get her when he was back. She stopped as she saw her father and knew he would be speaking with her.

Blackie reached her first, hugging her, then standing with his hands on her shoulders. "Finn? What's the word?"

"A concussion. Exposure. They've taken him for imaging, Caitlin said."

"Caitlin?" She looked up at Timothy. "Caitlin works here?"

Finn nodded even as she moved into her father's hug. "She does, Dad. After all

Mistletoe did to her, she couldn't leave the area."

Timothy wrapped his arms tight around his daughter and then drew her to a chair, looking up as Simon walked towards them.

"Simon?" Josh rose as Simon looked their way.

He nodded at an acquaintance across the room and then reached for the cup of coffee Josh handed him, grimacing at the bitter taste.

"How is Jacob?"

Finn looked up at him. "Concussion. Exposure. I've been back."

"And we need to talk about that, young lady." Timothy's voice was stern, even though compassion flooded his eyes. "You can't go around saying what I know you said."

"All I saw was that I was a good friend and he had no family." Finn stared among the men, a frown in place, not quite sure what their looks meant.

Timothy sighed, a prayer raising from his heart for healing for his young friend and protection for his daughter's heart. He also prayed that whatever it was that Jacob was seeking would be found quickly.

"Finn?" Simon stared at her, not quite sure what he should be asking her.

"All right. Fine. I said I was a close friend and that he had no family. They let me back. Caitlin's coming to get me when they bring him back from imaging." She stared at Simon, a frown on her face. "They didn't say much. A concussion. Exposure. That's all they will confirm."

Simon nodded as he set his cup down and rose. "Stay here, Finn. I'll see that you're banned from there unless you do." He stared her down until she looked away.

Finn sank back on her chair, her eyes following Simon as he walked away, not seeing Josh and Blackie sitting down on either side of her, her father sitting beside Blackie. Please, Lord, let Jacob be okay. And don't let Simon follow through on his threat. Josh and Blackie exchanged looks over her head before their eyes dropped to her face and the worry and devastation they could see there.

A hour later, Simon stood behind Finn as she watched from Jacob's bedside, an arm supporting her. She studied the man laying there, his eyes closed, his head tossing from side to side. She winced as she saw the large bandage that wrapped around his head, knowing it covered the wound he had been given.

"Did they say when they would let him go, Simon?"

"Maybe tomorrow. As long as Blackie is willing to help look after him." Simon drew her away. "We need to get you home, Finn. Josh and Blackie are waiting for you. Your Dad went on ahead."

She shook her head. "I don't want to leave him."

"Once again, Finn, you don't have a choice. You need to leave. We'll get you back here tomorrow." Simon steered her out the door and down to the hospital entrance. "What about your store?"

"Candy said she'd work it, but I can't let her." Finn sighed. "I don't know what I'll do."

"Work your store. I'll have someone let you know when you can come see Jacob. It may be he'll be well enough to go home."

Finn stood, shivering in the cool damp air, lost in thought, before she raised her eyes to Simon, finding him watching her.

"What do they want, Simon? What does Jacob have that they want?"

He shrugged, even as he tucked his hand into her arm to lead her to where Blackie stood waiting. "I don't know, Finn. I don't even know if Jacob knows. But I suspect it is something in one of those journals he's been reading. He tells me you've been reading them too."

She nodded. "I have been, but I feel so lost reading them. I don't know his grandparents, so I'm not sure what level of value to put on different thoughts or people's names. We've been making a list. Maybe I should see if Jacob will let you have a copy."

"We can address that later. I think he's already been talking with Blackie and Blackie's father about just that." Simon tucked her into Blackie's vehicle, then stepped back to where he could watch her.

"She's going to try and get back in overnight, you know that, Simon." Blackie's voice was quiet.

"She will, but make sure she doesn't. It won't do either one of them any good if she gets banned from him. And that's what will happen. Keep me updated on how he is? I'll try and stop in tomorrow at some point. I really need to hear what he has to say."

Blackie nodded. "I'll do just that."

Chapter 11

*H*is balance off, Jacob hesitated as he stepped through into his bedroom, Blackie's hand on his arm keeping him upright. He looked longingly at his bed but turned towards the bathroom, staggering sideways as he did so.

Blackie gave a small smile. "You need to get laying down, Jacob. With the concussion and vertigo, you can't be on your feet for long."

Jacob gave his friend a black look, even as his hand went to his abdomen. "No, I need to go in there." He pointed to the bathroom and moved cautiously that way. "I'm going to be sick and I don't want to be sick out here."

Blackie guided his friend to the room, then closing the door, walked back across to the hallway. It was evening and Jacob had just been released into his care. Finn hovered near the door, worry etched on her face.

"Blackie?"

"He'll be fine, Finn. It's to be expected he'd feel nauseous. Now, how be you find us some ginger ale, crackers, water, what have you that will sit easy on his stomach?"

She hesitated, her eyes on the room door, before she nodded. "I can do that."

"Give us about fifteen to twenty minutes. I need to get him settled and it won't be an easy task."

"Is he really okay, Blackie?" Finn watched Blackie's face.

"He is, Finn. He's had harder hits and worse injuries than this and survived."

She stared at him. "Worse than this? Oh, dear. I don't like the sounds of that."

Blackie laughed, turning her towards the stairs. "Go on. Find what I asked. Come back in twenty minutes."

Twenty minutes later, Finn stood outside Jacob's door, shifting from foot to foot, a tray in her hands, watching for the door to open.

Blackie stood for a moment, watching his friend. He had finally gotten Jacob settled, an ice pack on his neck, some painkillers down his throat, and now Jacob had drifted off. He sighed to himself. He had heard the soft footsteps outside the door and knew Finn was waiting for him. He stared at the door and then back at Jacob, trying to make up his mind what actually was going on with those two.

He turned towards the door and as he turned, he saw the papers Jacob had been working on. Jacob had muttered that he couldn't work on them, feeling like he was, and would Blackie take it on. Blackie hated to intrude that way, but he knew he had to. Someone was after his friend and he wanted it over yesterday and the culprit behind bars.

Finn watched as the door opened and Blackie slipped out, the tray shaking slightly in her hands. Blackie reached for it, setting it on the table in Jacob's room, before he reached to hug Finn.

"Blackie?" Finn's voice was muffled against him.

Blackie turned her back to the stairs and with an arm around her, led her back to their living area.

"He's sleeping now, Finn. He needs it. I'll have him awake a few times overnight, and I know that won't go over well."

"Who did this, Blackie?" Her eyes searched his, not seeing an answer.

"I don't know. Neither does Simon." Blackie stared down at the papers in his hands. "Jacob asked me to go over what he had found. I could use your help. You know the people in this town."

She nodded, even as she headed for the counter and mugs she had left sitting there. She filled them with tea and set Blackie's down in front on him before sliding into a chair and reaching for Aaron's journal.

"I've gone through his grandmother but not his grandfather's." She rose and headed back up the stairs, Blackie's eyes following her, before she ran back down, a notebook in her hand.

"Here. These are my notes." She sighed as she looked down at Aaron's journal. "I feel like I'm invading Aaron's privacy or something."

"Don't feel that way. I suspect Aaron knew Jacob would call in help." He pointed to the journal. "Now, read. I'm going to go over all your notes."

Three hours later, Blackie leaned back in his chair and stretched, reaching to gently take Aaron's journal from Finn. At her protest, he grinned.

"It's getting late, Finn, and you need to be in your store tomorrow. No, don't protest. That's where Jacob would want you. He'll likely sleep most of the next few days, and his body needs that."

She finally stood, stacking the papers, notebooks and journals into a neat pile and then handing them to him. "I'm not sure I accomplished anything tonight, but you can look through what I did. We need to find out what is actually going on. I think his grandfather left a clue or cryptic message somewhere in there." She paused, her hands reaching for the journal again, and she flipped through it to a sketched image. "I've seen this or something like it." She paused, her eyes growing round. "I have it in the store. I'll bring it home tomorrow night."

"That sounds like a plan. Good night, Finn." Blackie walked away, leaving her standing staring after him.

Finn stood in her store late the next morning, staring around. It had been a busy morning and she finally broken down and called in a friend to come and help her. She needed to hire someone to help with the Christmas rush, she decided. She had stood for a while, wrapped in her jacket, outside

133

watching the townsfolk and tourists rush through the day, carrying bags and packages she knew contained Christmas gifts. Her mother, she thought, would seen be baking her Christmas goodies and be after the three of her family to decorate the B&B for the holidays.

She headed for the office, a thought sidetracking her. She searched until she found the globe she was looking for, a small old-fashioned one, and picked it up, carrying it with her. She didn't remember where it came from and she had a good memory as to her stock. She sat, staring at it, realizing that Aaron had likely left it for Jacob just as he had left his wife's journal. It's a wonder it wasn't sold, Lord, but I can see Your hand in that, keeping it here for Jacob.

She looked up at a noise and saw Blackie and Simon standing in her doorway, grinning at her. She frowned.

"Blackie? Who's with Jacob?"

"Caitlin stopped by. She said she's a friend of yours?" At her nod, Blackie continued. "She offered to sit with Jacob for a while, to give me a break." He nodded at her desk. "You found it."

Simon stared between the two of them. "Found what?"

"This globe." Finn reached to hand it to him. "Here, you take it back to my place. I think it's dangerous for me to have." She looked between the two men. "It matches the etching, Blackie. We need to examine it closely."

"Why would that be so important?" Simon was puzzled.

Blackie took pity on him. "Finn found an etching in Aaron's journal last night. This globe matches it. I'm taking it back to the B&B and see if Jacob remembers it."

Simon reached for it, his hands running over it. He frowned. "There's a seam or something here, Blackie and Finn. I won't look at it too much closer until I can see the etching." He looked around. "Isn't it time for you to close up?"

Finn shot a glance at the clock and sprang from her chair. "It is. Just let me ring off the cash and stuff it into the safe." Simon followed her, eyes watchful as she quickly finished off her tasks, sending her friend on her way, and heading for the office with her cash.

"Do you need to deposit that tonight, Finn?" Simon's quiet question stopped her in her tracks.

She stared down at the money bag. "I should. I didn't do last night's either."

Simon sighed, pointing her to her chair. "Do your deposit and we'll walk you to the bank on your way home."

Finn glanced at him, then at Blackie, finding the two men sharing a glance. She rushed to do her deposit, sealing it into the bag and reaching for her coat. She turned to find Simon with the bag in his pocket, reaching for her keys.

"Set your alarm, Finn, and turn off all the lights you normally do. Let's get you home." He grinned at her frown. "Your mom asked us for supper and she said we would enjoy it. Something about stew and fresh bread."

Finn stood a while later at the open door to Jacob's room, her eyes on him, not seeing Caitlin standing behind her. Blackie watched her before he moved up beside her, his hand on her arm drawing her closer to Jacob.

"How is he really, Blackie?"

"He's groggy right now, Finn. It will take a few days until he can sit upright. Your mom has been feeding him when he's awake." He turned her away from the bed, his hand guiding her back out of the room.

She stood for a moment, looking back at Jacob. "Was it because of me this happened, Blackie?"

Blackie shook his head. "We don't know yet, Finn. It may well not have been. Simon and his people are still investigating."

Three hours later, Simon reached for the globe Finn was turning over and over in her hands as she read through Aaron's journal. She looked up, startled, meeting his grin.

"That won't solve anything, Finn." Simon studied the globe. "It has to open somehow, but I just can't figure it out."

Timothy reached for it. He had come in late from his construction work and had been sitting watching them. He examined the globe carefully, finally detaching the base from it. He rose, heading for the kitchen to find a pin or something. That should work, he thought. There's a small hole that if I do this correctly it will open the globe.

Finn could hear her brother and her parents talking in the kitchen, her brother breaking out into laughter at something his mother had said. She smiled, thanking God for her family, and then breathing a prayer for healing for Jacob. She heard an exclamation from Timothy and raised her head, watching as he walked back towards her, the globe in two halves.

"Dad! What did you just go and do?" Finn was shocked, even as she took the pieces of the globe he handed her.

"It's okay, Finn. It was meant to come apart. I think you'll find the contents interesting."

The three men crowded around, watching intently as Finn stared down at the globe before her fingers reached for the paper inside it.

She looked up. "Jacob should be the one reading this first, not us."

Blackie shook his head. "No, he would tell you to. Things like this aren't important to him. People are."

Finn finally reached for the paper, exclaiming as she uncovered a ring laying underneath it. She held up the ring, a ring containing five different gemstones.

"This is unique. I wonder if Jacob knows about it."

"Jacob knows about the ring. He just haven't seen it in years." Jacob startled them all by appearing in the room and then dropping down beside Finn on the couch, his head falling forward for a moment. He looked up, squinting against the light, as he reached for the ring. "This was my great great grandmother's. Grand showed it to me when I was a child but then I never saw it again. Grand, what were you up to?"

Finn handed him the letter, but he shook his head.

"You read it, please, Finn. I can't see well enough to follow any writing."

"You shouldn't be out of bed." She frowned as he gave a half-smile.

"Don't worry so much, Finn. I'll be okay." He jabbed at the paper she held. "Now read."

"If you're sure."

"I am."

Finn slowly opened the page, her eyes scanning it before she looked up, shock on her face.

Chapter 12

$\mathcal{J}$acob reached for Finn's hand. "Is it really that bad, Finn?"

"I'm not sure what to say, Jacob. It certainly explains a lot of things in this town but leaves a lot of questions as well." She stared at him for a moment, a question on her face, before she looked down. She didn't see her parents and brother edge into the room and sit where she couldn't see them. "Let me read it out loud."

"Charter for the formation of the town of Mistletoe:

"The following families have agreed among themselves to incorporate Mistletoe as a town, with the following stipulations:

"1. None of the land is to be sold to outsiders.

"2. Land possessed by these five families will be passed down to the males of each family. If there are no male issues, then the land passes to the females. If there are no issues for a family, the land will be held in perpetual trust by the remaining families.

"3. Land is to be purchased or acquired as needed for town expansion, with the land being divided among the families.

"Signed by the following families:

"Whitson, Bronagh, Blackwell, Gardner, and Smithson."

Jacob's hand stopped her. "That's all there is, isn't there?"

Finn nodded. "There is. It pretty much tells you what to do with the land."

"It does. If someone found this, they could destroy it, or use it to take control of the land. We would have to trace back the families."

Finn's hand stilled as she followed the paper. "That's what he meant."

"What who meant, Finn?" Blackie looked at Jacob before his glance went to Finn.

"Aaron. In the last few pages of his journal, he documented a visit to his lawyer. He didn't say why, but I would imagine the lawyer was tracing your families." She looked between Simon and Blackie. "How did you come to Mistletoe, anyway?"

Blackie shrugged. "Dad got a letter from a lawyer, suggesting we might want to check out Mistletoe. It didn't say why. I had never heard of the town before."

Simon leaned his head back as he studied the ceiling. "I received an offer of employment with the county force. I thought it was just in response to some feelers I put out." He glanced over at Jacob. "I have a feeling your lawyer was behind it." He looked over at Blackie. "Josh was offered the cafe."

"So it sounds as if all of us were brought back here at this particular time." Jacob rubbed at his forehead. His headache was back and he knew he'd soon have to deal with it.

"Jacob, let's get you back to your bed." Blackie stood, hauling Jacob to his feet. "We can deal with this tomorrow. Right now, we're all in too much shock to think clearly. And it is late."

Jacob nodded even as he wavered on his feet, Blackie's hand keeping him steady. They watched as he moved slowly back towards the stairs.

Jacob drew a deep breath as he contemplated the stairs, knowing he shouldn't have come down them.

"They're not going to bite you." Blackie grinned at the dark look Jacob sent his way. "Come on, friend. Let's get you up them."

Finn slowly folded the charter and then handed it to her father. "We need you to lock this and the globe in the safe, Dad. I don't think we should leave it out anywhere."

"No, that's not likely a good idea, love." Timothy headed for the office, pausing at the door. "You know we'll have to contact Jacob's lawyer. He likely has more information for us." He shook his head. "It's just strange the way Aaron did this. That globe could have been sold."

"I know, Dad. It's only God that kept it from happening." Finn turned to walk away, then spun back to stare at her father. "But the thing is, it wasn't there before. It only showed up after Jacob came to town. Did the lawyer bring it that day he came to meet with Jacob?"

Her father nodded. "That may well be what happened. We'll have to ask him." He glanced at the clock. "Right now, Simon needs to hit the road. Josh needs to get home so he can get up at his usual unearthly hour. You have a big day tomorrow too, Finn, with the sale you're planning."

❀ ❀ ❀ ❀ ❀

Finn looked up from her work the next morning, hearing her friend running towards her.

"Finn, get out of here. Gerry's back. I've locked the door. I hope you can get out the back door without him seeing you."

Finn stood. "Are you serious? He just can't stay away." She reached for her phone. "I'm not leaving. If he damages anything, I'll have him charged with that."

She spoke rapidly into the phone, for the first time getting a positive response. She frowned at her own as she turned to her friend.

"What happened to our police department? They never respond to me." She looked up as she heard sirens and saw Gerry looking around, before he once more began shaking the store door. "If he keeps that up, he'll break something."

Thirty minutes later, Finn walked back through her store, her hands rubbing up and down her arms, a frown in place. The officers who responded had promised her that Gerry would not be out again soon. There had been too many violations of his restraining order.

They had talked to the judge who ordered him into custody.

Anna looked around. "Well, at least he didn't scare off all the customers." She grinned at Finn's frown.

"No, thank goodness for that." Finn spun to study the door and then moved away to assess her stock. "Something is different, Anna. What is it?"

Anna finally pointed at the wrapped gifts Finn had placed under the tree. "Aren't there more there than yesterday?"

Finn knelt, sorting through them. "There are. Five to be exact." Her hand froze as she reached for them. "Anna, they have our names on them. All five of us. Simon, Josh, Blackie, Jacob, and I." She looked up, fear etching on her face. "Who put them here?"

Anna shrugged. "I have no idea. Do you think they're safe to open?"

"I don't know." Finn rose, heading for the storeroom, returning with a box. "I'll take them with me tonight and ask the guys."

Finn set the box down on the table in the living room at home and glared at Jacob, who sat in an easy chair near the fire, watching her.

"Why are you up?"

"Finn, back off. The doctor was here and okayed it. I can't stay flat until I recover."

She sighed as she slid down into a chair. "I know you can't. I'm just worried about you."

Jacob tilted his head to watch her. She was becoming important to him and he was learning to read her moods. "What happened today?"

"Why do you think anything happened?" She stared at him, finally giving a sigh. "Gerry Adams showed up today but at least the police dealt with him. Anna managed to get the door closed and locked before he entered the store." She glanced at the box. "After the police left, I felt something off in the store. I found these."

Jacob rose and walked carefully over to the table, peering into the box. "Christmas presents? That's not odd, is it?"

"No, not in itself. It's the fact that there is one for each of us."

"One for each of us?" Jacob carefully removed them from the box, setting the box on the floor out of the way. "They're all basically the same size, wrapped the same." He leaned over to read the tags, his hand balancing himself against the table. He frowned. "I don't get this. Why one for each of us? Who knew who we were and that we were here?"

"Your lawyer." Finn paced the living room, arms wrapped around herself. She was feeling afraid. "You need to talk to him and soon, Jacob."

He nodded, regretting that at the pain he felt. "I will. Tomorrow, I promise. Aren't you curious to see what yours is?"

She snorted. "You don't unwrap Christmas presents before Christmas."

"On the contrary, I think these are meant to be opened now." He reached for his phone laying on the side table by the chair he had been sitting in. "I need to call the others."

"I already have. Simon can't make it tonight nor can Josh. That leaves you, me and Blackie." She paused, her eyes on her father standing in the kitchen doorway. "Dad, what's your take on this?"

"My take on what? And why do you have Christmas presents out already?"

"Your take on these. Anna and I found them this afternoon under the store tree. There is one for each of the four guys and myself."

Timothy stood for a moment, his gaze going between the young couple in front of him before walking over to the table. "Do either of you recognize the handwriting?"

Jacob nodded. "I think it's Grand's lawyer but I'm not sure. No, wait. It's Grand's. Now how did he know all our names?"

"That's something that may be explained in the package, but you may also have to talk to your lawyer." Timothy paused, a thoughtful look on his face. "If it is your grandfather's, Jacob, then there is no reason not to open them. On the other hand, if you feel better having Simon go over them before you do, that's another option."

Finn stared at the box, finally reaching for the one labeled for her. "I'm going to open it. I need to know. I won't sleep unless I do." She carefully peeled back the paper, finding a small box inside. She frowned as she carefully opened it, finding a smaller box inside. She raised her eyes to the two men, her gaze lingering on Jacob who had moved closer to her.

When she finally opened the small box, she hesitated, finding what looked like a jewelled piece of puzzle. "Jacob? What is this?"

Jacob took it from her, turning it over and over, before he began laughing. Timothy and Finn stared at him.

"Jacob? Care to share?" Timothy's grin grew wider as Jacob's look of astonishment turned to wonder and then understanding.

"Let me open mine. I have an idea of what Grand was up to." He opened his box, taking out another piece of puzzle. Laying the two pieces down flat, he carefully worked them together. "This is a puzzle that Grand designed by the looks of it. It has to be something in this town. That's why he's drawn us all here."

Finn shook her head. "I have no idea what he would have been thinking. We'll have to wait until tomorrow when the others can make it out here." She looked at her father. "Dad?"

He threw up his hands even as he laughed. "I know. Put them in the safe. If you two keep on, I'll have to buy another safe just for your belongings."

Finn shook her head at her father before turning, finding Jacob watching her, a look on his face she couldn't read. Timothy watched the two of them, his heart raised in prayer. Lord, if this is the man You have chosen for our Finn, bless them. If not, protect both their hearts.

Simon, Blackie and Josh stared at Jacob the next night before their eyes went to Finn, who stood nodding and grinning at them.

"Puzzle pieces? Seriously?" Blackie reached for his package. "And it was your grandfather, Whit?"

"It was." Jacob nodded at the packages. "Go on. Open them. Then we'll see how they fit with ours."

An hour later, they all stood staring down at the assembled puzzle, no clearer as to its meaning. Finn frowned, a look crossing her face that Jacob wondered at.

Simon excused himself as his phone rang, walking away from them, spinning abruptly to stare at Finn. Josh watched him, then shook his head, looking back to the puzzle and listening to the wild ideas that were being tossed around.

Finn finally turned the puzzle over and stopped, her fingers tracing an etching on the back.

"Did you guys see this? It's a raised etching. Now, I wonder?" She ran for a piece of paper and a pencil, making a tracing of the etching, laying it flat on the table and flipping the puzzle back over. She looked up as Simon laid a hand on her shoulder. "Simon?"

"I have some news, Finn." He looked up at Jacob, who was watching intently. "Gerry Adams was killed last night in custody. We're investigating that. He won't be bothering you any more."

Finn backed away from Simon, stopping as she felt Jacob move behind her. "Murdered? Who? How?"

"I can't give any details yet, but yes, it was a murder. I'm sorry. I'll need to leave. Let me know what I can do to help with this puzzle."

Finn stood, stunned, unable to comprehend that the villain who had haunted her for so many years no longer would. She looked up at Josh and Blackie, not able to read the looks on their faces, before she turned to Jacob.

"Jacob?"

"Simon will find out, Finn. Leave it with him. Now, do we continue our research tonight, or do we do something fun?"

"Fun, after that news? How can we?"

Jacob reached to pull her into a hug. "Yes, fun. We need to get your mind off what happened." He turned her towards the lounge area at the front of the house. "Your mom asked if we would decorate tonight. Blackie and Josh will help." He looked over his shoulder, catching their nods. "We'll be done in no time."

"How be we tackle the outside and you two the inside? Bit of friendly competition and all." Blackie laughed at their expression, trying to lighten the mood for Finn.

She shrugged, her mind not on what she was doing. She just followed along behind them, reaching for the garland Jacob handed her for the dark wood mantle of the large fireplace.

She stopped an hour later, her hands clenching the ornaments she was holding before she set them down, a puzzled look on her face.

Jacob watched her walk away, his hands busy hanging the ornaments on the tree she had handed him. He turned as he heard the laughter from his friends as they came in.

"Where's Finn?" Blackie looked around. "We need her opinion on the lights."

Jacob nodded towards the living quarters. "Back there. I'm not sure what's up with her."

Blackie caught Finn up in a hug as she rushed back through the doors, spinning her in a circle before setting her down.

"Finn, you're in a rush. We need your opinion outside."

"It's fine." She didn't move towards the door or even look at them.

Blackie and Josh started laughing. "How can you say that when you haven't even seen it?"

She looked up, bringing her thoughts back to the room. "I've seen what Josh did at his place. He'll have done as nice a job here as there." She headed for Jacob, hooking an arm through his and drawing him away from the tree. She stopped, staring at the tree.

"I don't think we've ever had such a nice tree. Are you sure you three aren't interior decorators in disguise?"

Jacob shook his head, his hand resting on hers. "No. But what was the rush? You took off out of here so fast."

"I figured out what the etching is and where it is." She pointed to the map she now held. "There. About an hour past Pops' cabin. There's a set of hills that match this. There are also caves there. Could something be hidden in one of the caves? Could there be more hints in his journal?"

Jacob stared at her for a moment, then reached for the map she held. "This is the area?" When she nodded, he looked around, then laid the map on a table, the other two men crowding around them. Thankfully, he thought, there were no guests in the lounge at the moment. He stood staring down at the map, wondering just what his grandfather had been up to. He sighed as his phone chimed and excused himself.

"Norman? What's going on?"

Norman gave a soft laugh. "Don't you remember the scavenger hunts you and your grandfather used to dream up? He said this was an adult version of it. You'll have more information tomorrow. I'm taking it you found the gifts."

"We did. When did you put them there?"

"I didn't. Someone in town did for me. No, I'm not saying who is was. But that's not why I called. We need to meet again. You have some decisions to make. You haven't settled down into your work again and your Grand would want you to."

Jacob sighed, thinking of his graphics company he had started. "I know. I'm getting there. It's just, just….." His voice died away.

"I know. It's tough without your grandfather to see and approve what you're doing, isn't it? Just be very careful, Jacob. Someone will try and stop you, even to the point of murder, from finishing off this hunt. I have heard rumours from the town, but no one can or will say who it is. Take care of your lady, too." With that, Norman was gone.

Jacob pocketed his phone, turning to watch Finn interact with his friends. He had to admit it, Norman was right. He was beginning to think of her as his lady, and he couldn't. He didn't have the right to do that. Lord, I have no idea what the next few days will bring, but You do. Protect us please. Keep my Finola safe.

Josh approached him. "I need to get going. Is everything okay?"

"It is, I think. Norman wants to meet. He said someone in town put out the packages for him but he wouldn't say who. Watch your back, Josh."

"I will. You watch yours and Finn's. She's come up with a plan to have her brother watch her store on Saturday and head out to the hills and the caves she says are there."

"I don't like that."

"Like it or not, you're not stopping her, you know." Josh laid a hand on his friend's shoulder and then headed out the door.

Jacob draped an arm over Finn's shoulders as he studied the map, not catching her quick intake of breath or Blackie's surprised look.

"When are you planning on this trip, Finn?"

"Saturday, I think. Peter will watch the store, I know, he and Anna. They like working together. From what I can remember, it's maybe an hour or less to the last of the caves, so we should be able to search them all." She looked up at him. "I just have no idea what we're looking for. Do you?"

Jacob shook his head, a thought crossing his mind. "Not off hand. I don't know about this, though, Finn. Something tells me it's too dangerous."

She glared at him as she hurried gathered up her papers. "Too dangerous?"

She spluttered for a moment, then turned and stalked away, leaving him staring after her.

"That went well, Whit." Blackie moved to stand beside him.

"I know, didn't it? Norman says we're all in danger from someone but he can't say who. I don't want to put her in any more danger."

Blackie shook his head as he walked away. "It's too late, Whit. She's determined to go, with or without us. Let's make sure we're with her."

Chapter 13

*S*aturday morning, Jacob shrugged into his backpack, his eyes searching the area. He didn't feel like they were alone. It almost felt as if someone was following them, but Simon hadn't said anything about that, and he knew Simon had been watching. He turned to watch Finn as she laughed at the nonsense Blackie was saying, her face alight. He wondered again at how beautiful she was, catching her eye as she turned to find him.

Thirty minutes later, Finn stopped, pointing to an area just off to their right. "There's the first cave. It's not really big, more like a depression. We can take a look at it, thought." She had shed her jacket, waving aside Jacob's concern, stating it was warm for that time of year but yes, the weather could change. She had searched the sky when she said that and then shook her head, saying it would likely stay nice for the rest of the day.

Blackie nodded to Simon. "We'll look it over. Anything in particular you would think we should be looking for?"

Jacob shot a look at Finn, then spoke. "Anything out of the ordinary. Maybe Finn should go with you. She's familiar with the caves. You are, aren't you, Finn?"

She nodded. "This is Pops' land, so Peter and I played here all the time. We know those caves well." She held up a camera. "We'll take pictures of every angle we can and have Peter and Dad take a look at them. They may see something we miss."

"Now that's thinking." Josh grinned at her before the three moved away. "How many caves are there, Jacob?"

Jacob shrugged. "Timothy said six. If we don't get to them all today, we'll come back. I want to be out of here before dark."

"I agree with you there." He turned as the three returned. "That was quick."

"Finn was right, it was small." Simon nodded towards the trail. "How far to the next one and is it any bigger?"

"About ten minutes and yes it is somewhat bigger but not as big as the last one. They all seem to increase in size." She looked around, suddenly nervous. "I don't know if we'll be able to explore the last one today. It's large and has some rooms off the main room. We'll likely have to come back to that one."

"Can we do that after church tomorrow?" Josh glanced at the other three men, catching their nods.

Finn shook her head. "I can't. It's the annual seniors' Christmas dinner at the church and I have to serve. Peter could come with you." She paused, her focus on the distance. "That might be the best idea. He's the one who really explored that last cave. I never liked it."

They had reached the last cave and Finn stood, rubbing her hands up and down her arms. She really didn't want to go into the cave, but she knew she had to. Jacob stood beside her, finally turning her so he could hug her.

"You don't have to go in, Finn. We'll take lots of pictures."

She shook her head. "I have to. There's just something about this cave I've never liked and I don't know why." She moved away, pulling out her flashlight and turning it on as she entered the cave, ducking to miss the top of the entrance. The four men followed her, eyes searching for what, they weren't sure of. She wrinkled her nose at the smell of animals and decay and death in the cave. Maybe that's what she hated about it, she thought

Blackie and Josh moved off towards one of the side rooms, leaving Jacob and Simon studying the main room and taking their photos. Finn finally moved away towards a room on the left, tired of waiting for the men. She knew she was leaving them on the other side of the cave and that scared her, but she was determined to overcome her fear.

She stood for a moment at the entrance, flashing the light around, trying to see if something just jumped out at her. This is ridiculous, she thought, now isn't it, Lord? Whatever it is will not just walk over and hit me over the head. She moved forward, her foot catching for a moment on what she thought was a rock.

Sudden sound and light filled the cave as an explosion ripped through the wall near Finn. She was flung forward into the room as the debris blocked off the entrance. The four men were thrown to the ground. Silence gradually filled the cave as the dust and smoke filtered out the entrance. No one moved.

❀ ❀ ❀ ❀ ❀

Four hours later, Timothy, Peter and other members of the town search and rescue group slowly approached the cave. Peter had called his father when Finn hadn't reported in three hours previously. They had decided as a group to go searching and this was the last cave.

Timothy's hand came to rest on Peter's arm.

"I don't like this, Peter. There's fresh debris near the entrance." He looked around, worry etched on his face.

"There is, Dad. I don't think they made it out." He turned to the other five with them. "Let's go, guys. Let's see what we're facing."

Slowly entering the cave, they stood for a moment, shocked at the destruction they saw. Hearing faint moans, they turned to the right, finding Simon and Jacob, and then further back, Blackie and Josh. No Finn.

"Where's Finn?" Timothy spun, trying to find his daughter, his eyes landing on the fresh rock pile. "No! Tell me it's not true!" He ran for the rocks, Peter on his heels.

Ed, one of their team members, was at their side. "Careful, guys. Start at the top.

We don't know where she is and we don't want to bring anything more down." He turned as he heard voices behind him. "Peter, go see if one of the men know where she is."

Two hours later, Peter stood in the room Finn had been entering. They had removed the debris, but had not found her. She had simply vanished. He frowned. There had to be another entrance, he thought, turning as he heard footsteps approaching. Jacob stood there, fear on his face for Finn.

"Where is she, Peter?"

"I have no idea, Jacob. There has to be another entrance here somewhere, but I don't see one. She can't have just vanished into thin air." He turned. "We'll need to come back tomorrow. First, we need to get you four checked out."

"We're fine, Peter. I'm staying at your grandfather's cabin tonight, even if I have to break into it." Jacob stared at Peter, silent communication going on between the two of them before Peter nodded.

"That's what I was planning. Dad's heading out with the rest. He knows that's what I was planning on doing. She has to be here somewhere, Jacob. I just don't see it."

Three days later, Jacob sighed as he signed into his laptop. He needed to work. He had clients waiting for graphics he was to be designing for them, but his heart wasn't in it. He stared at the screen as it flickered to life but what he saw was the cave and the rock pile. Peter and he had gone back to the cave the next day and the next day, searching for a secondary entrance, but finding nothing. Peter thought he had found a crack in the wall in the one room where Finn had been headed but neither one of them had been able to open it. They had searched around outside for a secondary entrance but again had drawn a blank.

He finally shook his head and pulled up his program. His email was overloaded, he thought. He sighed. He really didn't want to be this busy but it seems as if the Lord had other ideas. He was soon immersed in his work.

Mary came looking for him just after noon, having called him and gotten no response. She stood for a moment watching before heading back down for a tray of food.

Jacob didn't stir except to say a quiet thank you when she placed the tray next to him. Her hand rested on his shoulder for a moment before she walked away, her heart raised in prayer for the young man who had become so important to them all and such a part of their lives in so short a time.

Blackie stopped at Jacob's door later that day, finally bringing Jacob back to the present. He rose and stretched, his eyes going to the time.

"Blackie? Any word?'

Blackie shook his head. "We've been out with the search and rescue teams and a couple of dog trackers, but nothing. She's vanished into thin air. The last scent the dogs got was in that room."

"Then, where is she?"

Blackie shrugged, before he held out a shallow tin box. "I found this in the cave today. I think it's what we were looking for. I haven't opened it today. You can see where it was damaged by the explosion."

Jacob took it, turning it over and over, before setting it on his desk. He looked up. "Do we open it or do we wait?"

"I'd say we open it. We can share with the others what we find. I have a feeling time is short."

Jacob nodded, his hands shaking as he pried open the box. He stopped, staring at the parchment within, before looking up at Blackie.

"Blackie?"

"I don't know, Jacob. That looks old."

Jacob nodded, carefully handling the fragile parchment. He opened it and read it several times, his mind not comprehending what it all said. Blackie read over his shoulder, a soft exclamation coming from him.

"That would explain what your Grandfather was after then, wouldn't it?"

Jacob nodded before placing the parchment back into the box and picking it up to head for the stairs. He gave a quick grin. "Wonder if Timothy has invested in that other safe yet?"

Blackie started to laugh. "He'll have to soon, you know."

Chapter 14

*H*er eyes blinking open and closed, Finn slowly stirred, glancing around. She wasn't at home, she knew. She just didn't know where she was. She felt a hand under her head, holding it up to help her drink, then a cloth gently wiping away the spilled water. Her vision faded as she lost consciousness again.

The man stood watching her for a moment after straightening back up. The tin mug clanged slightly as he set it down on the rickety crate beside the rough bunk she was laying on. He looked around. He couldn't let her stay here. He had to get her away. He didn't know that it was Finn the man wanted him to guard, or he wouldn't have agreed to it. He wouldn't leave her here.

He crept to the door of the ramshackle house near the edge of Mistletoe, hidden back in the trees, and looked around. The man had left earlier, saying he would be back by noon. He glanced up at the sky. He had time to get her to his truck and to help. He turned as he heard a faint moan and then a cough from her, creeping back on silent feet before reaching to sweep her into his arms and out of the house, towards the truck he had hidden nearby. He carefully fastened her in and then stood for a moment, head cocked to listen before he slid behind the wheel. Surprisingly, the truck started right away and was almost silent. He had kept it that way.

He pulled to a stop near Finn's home, watching the activity going on around it. He needed to get her in there, but he'd have too many questions to answer if he walked in the front way. He stepped from the vehicle and walked around to the passenger door, scooping Finn into his arms and heading for the back door. He had been there frequently. Finn and her family treated him right, he decided.

Mary frowned at the tap at the back door. No one should be there, she thought. She pulled the door open, ready to tell off whoever was there, then stopped short, astonishment on her face. Old Jack, as he was called, stood in front of her, Finn in his arms. She reached to draw him in.

"Jack?"

"I found her, Miz Mary. I was to watch her for someone, but I just couldn't. You've been too good to me." Tears streaked down his face as he stared at her.

"Jack! Thank you! Timothy!"

Timothy came through the doors on the run at the urgency in his wife's voice, Peter on his heels, both men sliding to a stop as they saw Jack and Finn. Timothy reached for his daughter, tears on his own face, even as Peter reached out a hand and drew Jack to the kitchen table, seating him. Peter watched as his parents headed for the stairs. He knew they wouldn't take her to the hospital. Not now. Maybe later, once Doc had seen her.

Blackie peeked through the door and then came in, his eyes on Old Jack, who cringed away from him. He slid onto a chair away from Jack and just watched, a quiet work of thanks for the mug of coffee Peter handed him.

"Jack, when did you last eat?" Peter looked around from the fridge.

Jack shrugged, even as Jacob walked in, a puzzled look on his face. "Don't rightly remember, Peter. Not yesterday. Maybe not the day before."

"Then, a feast you will have. I remember you like Mom's breakfast casserole and bacon. I have that here for you.

Toast as well?" He slid a large mug of black coffee in front of the man, not waiting for an answer.

Jacob stood for a moment, not quite sure what was going on. He could hear hurried footsteps over head and then a new voice speaking from the front area. "Peter?"

Peter turned as he set the plate down in front of Jack. "Jack here found Finn. Mom and Dad are with her."

Blackie laid a hand on Jacob's arm. "Let them be with her. You'll get a chance, Jacob. Sit. Peter had tea for you." His eyes were on Jack. "What part of the service, Jack?"

Jack looked up, a startled look on his face, then fear tracing over it. "Who are you and why do you want to know?"

Blackie held up his hands. "Hey! No reason. I just recognize a brother vet is all. I was a medic in the armed forces."

Jack studied him, then turned his eyes to Jacob. "And you, what were you?"

"An MP." Jacob stopped him from rising. "That part of my life is over. I don't arrest or contain anyone any more. You're with friends here. May I call you Jack? I'm Jacob and this is Blackie."

The three men finally watched as Jack rose without saying a word when he was finished eating and walked out the back door.

"What's his story, Peter?" Jacob turned to watch the stairs even as he asked.

"He lives outside of town. We really need to do something about his house. It's almost falling down. But anyway, he's an army vet. Been living here for twenty years I think. He doesn't say much. Won't say if he has a family or not. Maybe you could check that out, Blackie."

"Why doesn't he live in town? He seems like a nice enough fellow." Jacob turned his eyes to Peter.

Peter shook his head. "Some people in town are real friendly to him, but then he's not real friendly to them. He does odd jobs around town, earning enough for food and whatnot. He has never said anything about his service, but Doc says he lives out there because he has really bad nightmares and doesn't want to scare anyone, especially the little ones. Doc checks in on him every week as do we."

"PTSD?" Blackie's question caught Peter's attention.

"That's what we think. It's never been confirmed though. He refuses all help."

They turned as footsteps sounded on the stairs and Timothy appeared, slumping down onto a chair. He thanked his son for the mug of coffee Peter set in front of him, his head bowing before he reached for the mug.

"Dad?"

Timothy looked up, his eyes on his son. "She's fine, son. Bumps, bruises. Doc says Jack looked after her well the last day or so. He's not sure where she's been before that though. He doesn't think Finn will remember though." He sighed. "He's afraid of pneumonia. She's doing some coughing. But he says all things considered she's in good shape. He doesn't think there are any internal or head injuries. He'll have to wait until she wakes up fully to assess for any memory loss or anything, he said."

Jacob stared at his hands. "If we hadn't gone there, she wouldn't have been hurt."

Timothy shook his head. "Whoever it is takes advantage of where you five are. He's likely watching you. He may even be listening to us without us knowing that. Simon's checked our place and says it's fine. He's also rechecked Finn's store."

Blackie watched the emotions flickering across Jacob's face and shared a look with Peter. "Jacob, any more thoughts on that parchment?"

Jacob brought his thoughts back to the room. "That puzzles me, Blackie. I don't get it."

"What parchment?" Peter hadn't heard about their find.

"We found an old tin box with a parchment in it. It must have been jarred loose from somewhere during the explosion." Jacob looked at Timothy, who nodded and rose, returning with the box. "We can't figure it out though. We're hoping Finn can help." He opened the box and carefully handed the fragile parchment to Peter.

Peter laid it down carefully and then opened it, staring at it for a moment, before he rose and headed for the library, returning with an old volume.

"Pops had this book. I think it was his father's, grandfather's, something like that. This parchment reminds me of something in there." Peter searched through the book, finding laying the book beside the parchment. "There. These almost match. It's the old homestead of the Whitsons, Dad. Out near Pops cabin. Jacob owns that now."

"I do? I didn't know I had property that close to yours." He rose and stood behind Peter, staring at the picture. "What is this?"

"It's an old mill, I think, Jacob. Your property contains a river with rapids and there used to be a flour mill there. Not big, just enough for the community. There is still some of the foundation there."

"There is, Peter. I was out there about a month ago, just checking on the property, like I've always done. There's not a lot of the foundation left, but we can check it out."

Jacob shook his head. "You need to stay here with your daughter. Simon and Josh will be free on Saturday. We'll go then."

"Don't wait too long, or you'll be tracking through snow." Peter grinned at the look on Blackie's face. "Not sure about the snow, Blackie?"

"No.   I've always lived in warm climates, although being the armed forces did take me to some colder places."

Jacob started to laugh. "Nothing like here, though, Blackie. Nothing like here."

Timothy nodded as he rose. "Just be very careful wherever you go. Someone is after you four and Finn as well. I've heard rumours in town, but I can't pin them down to anyone in particular. The townsfolk are not too sure about you young men. You're newcomers to town, even though your roots are here. Finn, they'll watch out for."

Turning her head slowly, Finn roused, her eyes peeping open as she looked around. Surprised to see her own room, she sat up, regretting it as the room spun and she dropped back to her pillow. Hearing movement to her side, she jumped, then relaxed as she realized it was Peter.

"Finn. You're awake. Here. Doc wants you to drink lots." He held a glass of juice for her to sip.

"Peter? How'd I get here? The last I remember was standing outside Pops' cabin."

"Old Jack brought you home. He's not saying much about where he found you." Peter sat on the edge of her bed, leaning back on a hand. "You really don't remember?"

She shook her head. "No. Tell me, What happened?"

"You and the four guys were exploring the caves behind Pops. In the last one, somehow an explosion was triggered and you were supposed to be trapped in one of the rooms. Only you weren't there when we got through the debris." He studied her face. "You really don't remember at all?"

"No. The guys are okay?"

Peter grinned. "Yes, Jacob is." He ducked back as she swiped at him. "They're all fine. Just bumps and bruises. Jacob and I kept going back to look for you." He studied her. "I wish you could remember. There had to be another entrance to that room."

"Was it the first one on the left when you walked into the cave?" At his nod, she continued. "Pops showed me the door one time. It leads back to the other side of the hill. About a mile or so I think."

"That's why we couldn't find it then. But you wouldn't have been there anyway. Jack's not saying much."

"What time is it?"

"About two in the morning. One of us has been with you since Jack brought you home yesterday morning."

"What day is it?"

"It's Wednesday morning. Why?"

She groaned. "I have a new client coming in with some objects for the consignment shop. I have to be there today."

"Not happening, sis. I'll meet him. Luke's okay with me being off this week." Peter worked for a local contractor.

"That's not the same, Peter. I need to see the pieces."

"Then, how be I take you down there long enough to meet with him and then bring you back home? Other than that, you call him and postpone."

She finally nodded, her eyes closing. "He's due to be there for 10. Wake me about 8:30. I'll need time to get ready. I'm not moving very fast, am I?"

Peter gave a low laugh. "No, you're not. It's a good thing Jacob had to travel last night to meet with his lawyer today. He'd have something to say about your plans."

"Really? I don't think it will matter to him what I do." Her breath evened out as she slept.

Peter sat for a few minutes, watching his sister, just one year younger than him. They had always been best friends, never a real argument between them. He finally shook his head as he rose and then dropped a kiss on her cheek. "But it will, Finn. It will. You don't see the way he looks at you, his heart in his eyes. Please, God, don't let her get hurt by a guy again. But somehow, I think you brought Jacob into her life for a reason. Please, let him stay. She needs him and he needs her.

He turned as he felt an arm around him. Mary stood there.

"She's been awake?"

"She has, Mom. She's planning on going to the store tomorrow. She has a new client to meet."

"I don't like that, but it is her choice, Peter. One of us will be with her."

"I told her I would take her and then bring her home." He stooped to kiss his mother on the cheek. "I'm off to bed then, Mom, if you're here." He stopped on his way to the door, turning to find his mother watching him. "What's Jacob going to say?" He grinned as she shook her head.

"He's not going to be happy, I know, but he's just a friend. So far, anyway."

Chapter 15

*J*acob stared at Mary, not quite sure he had heard her right. "She's where?"

"You heard me, Jacob. She's at her shop. She had to meet a client this morning. No matter how sick she is, her clients come first. This is a new one to her, with antique documents that she wants to put up."

Jacob shook his head. "It's that important to her? More important than her health?"

Mary's anger grew and she drew Jacob to the table, shoving him down in a chair. He looked at her in shock as she sat beside him, her hand on his arm.

"You need to be very careful how you treat Finola, Jacob. She looks strong but she has a very fragile side, one she has shown you. She doesn't show this to very many people, other than the ones she loves, and that would basically be her father, her brother and me. Pops and her had a special relationship. You also need to understand that when she was about twelve, she was beaten severely and left lying in an abandoned house. She can't remember who did it or if she does, she's buried it too deep to bring out. Pops is the one who found her. She hadn't come home and we started to look for her. I'll never forget the look on his face the day he walked in with her in his arms. It crushed him, Jacob. She's been afraid to let people close since then. That tells us it was someone she knew well who did it."

"And you have no idea who?"

Mary shook her head, compassion for the young man in her eyes. "We don't. We might suspect someone but we have no proof." She pointed at him. "Today, this was her way of claiming back her life. She wasn't ready to go to the store, far from it, but she had made a commitment to someone and she always keeps her word. Anna has taken up a lot of the slack for her. Peter and Anna are a couple, if you missed that, and Anna really wants to go into the store with Finn, if Finn will have her. She's been learning a lot, taking courses over the internet, with that in mind. It was God's way of having someone prepared to take over for Finn."

Jacob nodded, his mind slowly digesting what Mary had told him. "I'll be careful with her, Mary. I don't want to hurt her."

"We know you don't, Jacob, but you didn't know her history. She wouldn't have told you, not thinking it necessary. That would have left you doing or saying something that would have frightened her deeply and chased her away from here."

"I can see that. In ways, we're both walking wounded, aren't we? I lost my parents when I was young, and then Grams when I was ten, eleven, something like that. I lost buddies overseas." He paused, his eyes on his folded hands. "Believe me, I don't want to hurt her."

Mary stood, hugging him, and then dropping a kiss on his forehead. "We know you won't. Just don't tell her I told you. She needs to trust you enough to tell you herself. It will come with time."

She looked up as the door opened and Finn and Peter walked in. Finn stumbled as she tried to take off her boots. With an exclamation, Peter swept his sister up into his arms and headed for the stairs, shaking his head at his mother, Finn's arms around his neck, her head on his shoulder, eyes closed.

"I'll be right back. She overdid it, I think."

"I'm sure she did. There's fresh water and juice in her room, Peter. Make sure she takes some pain meds."

"I will, Mom. Be right back."

Jacob slowly sat back down, his eyes on the stairs, not knowing that his heart was showing to Mary. She gave a sad smile, knowing that Finn may well never think of Jacob that way and she hated to think that Jacob's heart would be broken.

Peter hugged his mother on the way by to the fridge. He pulled out sandwiches she had fixed and then reached for juice.

"Peter?" His mother stood beside him as he sat, her arm on his shoulders.

"She shouldn't have gone out, Mom. She couldn't even speak to Anna, she was that tired and in pain. I think we'll need to take her to the hospital. Doc thought we might have to."

"But what happened today, Peter?" Jacob's quiet voice broke into the silence that followed.

"She didn't meet with the client. Anna and I wouldn't let her. He was bizarre. He didn't have any antiquities, just a bunch of garbage. Anna looked at it and sent him on his way. Do you know when she set up the meeting?"

Mary shook her head. "No, I don't. She hadn't mentioned it. You don't think….." Mary's voice died away.

"They were trying to nab her again, weren't they, Peter?" Jacob had to tamp down his anger. "When will they leave her alone?"

"Not until we figure out who it is and what they want. And that answer I think lies on your property, at that old mill." Peter shared a look with Jacob. "Did your lawyer have any more information?"

Jacob shook his head. "Not really. He had no idea Grand was going to do this. He would have talked him out of it if he had. He doesn't want any more of us hurt. The thing is, we don't know what the answer is or why someone is after us if we don't follow through."

"I can tell you what they're after." Finn spoke from the bottom of the stairs. Her face was white and Jacob noted the dark circles under her eyes. "That man today, Peter? He used to live here. I don't think you know him, though. His son was in some of my classes during high school."

"That's why he looked so familiar then." Peter's hand steadied his sister as she sat. "You shouldn't be up."

"I need to be. I can rest when we solve this. You said something about the old mill?"

"Blackie found an old tin box with a parchment in it. It leads us to the old mill on Grand's property. We're planning on going out there on Saturday. And no, you're not coming." Jacob watched her closely.

Finn glared at him. "You can't keep me away, Jacob. I've as much invested in this now as you do. Someone tried to kill us all and that someone kidnapped me."

"Finn!" Jacob's voice was firm

"I'm not one of your prisoners, Jacob. Get that through your head. If you are all going, so am I. Peter? Are you in?"

Peter quickly hid a smile, seeing his mother doing the same. "I can't, Finn. Anna wants me to help her with the store."

"That figures. Copping out, aren't you?" She stood, wavering for a moment, waving off the hands that came out to steady her. She turned to Jacob, a hurt look on her face. "At least with you, I thought I had a friend and an ally. You're just like all the rest, aren't you? See a female and think you have to protect, regardless of the circumstances or even if the female is able to protect themselves." She stopped herself from continuing, glaring at him. "Stay away from me, Jacob. I don't need any more people like you in my life." She turned and walked away, leaving him standing staring after her.

Jacob's eyes never left the stairs as he sank back into his chair, Mary's and Peter's eyes in turn on him. Peter shook his head as he met his mother's eyes and a small smile appeared on her face.

"This is what I meant, Jacob. She's begun to trust you and doesn't understand that you care too much for her to see her hurt. You need to talk to her." Mary's hand rubbed his back. "She'll come around. Just don't shut her out. We've never coddled her, wrapped her in cotton and stuck her on a shelf because she's female. She won't accept you doing that." Jacob had turned to her. "I have no idea who is after you five, but someone is. And one of you right now is in real danger. I sense that. It's you or Finn, I can't determine which one of you it is."

"And Mom usually can do that." Peter picked up their dishes and headed for the sink. "Talk to her, Jacob. But first, spend time in prayer. Decide exactly what she means to you." He turned to face his friend.

"I'm getting the sense that she's important to you. Tell her that if that's the case. She won't throw it back into your face. She treasures your friendship. I've seen her let you do things not even we can do for her."

Jacob nodded, his eyes flickering between the two and then to the stairs. "If I go up there now, will she talk to me?"

Mary spoke up, her hand on Jacob's arm keeping him in his chair. "Not just yet. Give her a couple of hours. You need to spend those hours with God. Talk to her then. You also need to deal with your business. You can't let it slide."

Jacob looked down, blinking rapidly to clear his eyes. He had never had a woman talk to him like that, not even his own mother or his Grams. "Thank you, Mary. I'll do just that."

Finn looked up later that afternoon as she felt the couch sink beside her. Jacob sat there, his eyes on the fireplace, not on her. She tilted her head to study him and opened her mouth to speak but didn't when he reached for her hand.

Jacob entwined their fingers, his eyes on her neat nails, before he frowned. "You have presents on your nails."

She laughed. "I do. It's my one extravagance every once in a while. I get my nails done, particularly near special holidays. I'm sorry, Jacob. I shouldn't have said that to you."

"No. You were right when you said what you did. I want to protect you and that's me. Your mom talked to me and explained how it is with you, from their standpoint. So did Peter." He finally shifted to watch her face, finding her eyes on him. "I've begun to think of you as someone special in my life, Finn, and that scares me. I've never had a special lady before, just never found one, or had God direct me to one. You're that one."

She sighed. "I know, Jacob. I find it difficult to get to know people. I keep things in. It goes back to something that happened when I was young, when I was beaten up and left by myself. I can't remember who it was, but they think it's someone I trusted. I wish I knew who it was." She stopped at the pressure of his fingers on hers.

"That doesn't matter, Finn, not with me. You've shown you've trusted me right from the first moment we met."

She nodded. "Can we say we had the rest of this conversation and be done with it?"

Jacob began to laugh even as he pulled her into a hug. "We can. But I reserve the right to come back to it at some point."

She nodded, her hair brushing against his cheek. "I'll grant you that. That's something I never do either. Once a conversation is over, with me, it's over."

"Now what, Finn? You are really determined to go with us on Saturday?"

She stared at the fireplace. "I need to, I think, Jacob. Part of me is afraid to go, afraid of getting hurt again. Part of me is angry that we were in that explosion and all of us suffered to some extent." She looked back at him. "Part of me wants to run as far from this town as I can, and I know I can't do that. Does that make sense?"

"It makes perfect sense. It's how I feel." He settled back against the couch, his arms still cradling her to him. "I want this over, Finn. I never dreamed when I walked through this town that day how my life would be changed by it, how it would come to feel so much like home. I'm going to find one of Grand's properties and fix it up to live in. I can work from here."

"That would be nice, Jacob." She settled down against him, not seeing her father standing in the doorway behind them, watching intently before he moved on to find Mary.

They sat in silence for a while before Finn spoke, asking him about his lawyer.

"Norman? He's been Grand's lawyer for the last ten years or so. He took over for his uncle. Why?"

"Just how much do you trust him? How well do you know him?"

Jacob stilled, catching what she wasn't saying. "I see what you mean. I'll need to look into him, won't I? I'll call Blackie's Dad. He'll look into it for me, without letting Blackie know. The fewer of us in on this the better."

Chapter 16

Saturday found Jacob standing on his grandfather's property, looking around. He walked towards the cabin, finding it in surprisingly good shape. He tried the door, finding it locked, disappointed he couldn't enter. He felt Finn's hand on his, closing his fingers over something. He looked down as he opened his hand. A key. He looked up, seeing her smile and then her nod towards the door. He unlocked it, and shoved it open, still hesitating. He didn't see the looks of his three friends. Instead, he reached for Finn's hand, drawing her with him into the cabin. He sighed. He was just as he pictured it would be. His grandfather had built this dream cabin for him as a bedtime story when he was tiny. This was the cabin. He felt like he had come home.

Finn reached to wipe the tear from his face and he caught her hand again as he turned in a circle.

"You've kept it up for him, haven't you?"

Finn nodded. "Pops made us promise to do just that, just in case Aaron ever came back. He missed his friend so much." She looked around, seeing the other three men standing just inside the doorway, compassion on their faces for their friend. "Do you think he left anything here?"

Jacob shook his head. "I have no way of knowing. I think we need to look for the mill first and then come back here." He turned, stopping to study his friends. "I can't contact Norman. He's not answering his phone and his secretary has been taking my messages. I find that strange."

"It is strange, Jacob. Do you trust him?" Blackie spoke up.

"Finn asked me that the other day. I had your father research him. It's not what I expected to hear from your dad, what he reported. Apparently Norman is just one complaint short of being charged by the authorities. I don't know how Grand trusted him."

Blackie nodded. "I thought you'd check him out at some point. Now, where do we go from here, Finn?"

She pointed behind them. "Out the door, for starters." She smirked at their collective groan. "Lock up, Jacob. We sometimes have people coming through who shouldn't." She led the way across the clearing and stopped. "If we follow the path, it will take us to the remains of the mill. It's about a half mile, I think."

Simon moved to the front. "We want you between us, Finn. Blackie, you're on the end, Jacob, Finn, and then Josh behind me. No arguments, Finn, or we turn around and leave."

"I wasn't about to argue. I was going to say I appreciate your attention to my safety."

Simon shot her a suspicious look, finding her looking at him with understanding. He shrugged. "Okay, then. Let's move. I'd like to be out of here before dark." He glanced at the sky. "Those are snow clouds."

Finn shook her head. "Maybe, maybe not."

They stopped as they reached the river, hearing the rapids before they saw them. Jacob turned in a circle, studying the area. "This is on Grand's land?"

"It is, Jacob. He has about 30 acres of woodland here. This used to be the flour mill." Finn walked towards some of the large

stones that had formed the mill. "I guess
there was an explosion from the flour and that
destroyed the mill. After that, they took their
wheat to a neighbouring mill."

"Why would Grand send us here? I
don't see anything that would have him doing
that."

"Let's separate and look around. Finn,
stay with Jacob." Blackie headed off to his
left, his eyes searching for anything that
looked suspicious. Then he groaned. How
would he know what was suspicious,
anyway? He shot a glance around him and
saw the other four moving around, searching
as well.

Jacob moved towards the river, his eyes
on a large section of wall. He traced the
stones with his hands, Finn keeping step with
him. He finally stopped, his hands brushing
away debris and light snow, his fingers
tracing lettering.

"Did you know this was here, Finn?"

"What was here?"

"This." Jacob drew her to him, an arm
around her. "Look. It's a verse. 'Seek the
Lord while He may be found.' Grand used to
quote that to me at least once a day." He
looked up, blinking away tears. "I think we

found the treasure, Finn. Let's go find the others."

Finn looked around. "But where are they? They can't have disappeared."

Shards of stone flew through the air, and Jacob caught Finn in his arms, taking her down and shoving her against the stone, covering her as best he could with his own body.

Finn struggled to get away from him, but he only pressed her tighter to the ground. "Jacob! Let me up!

"Ssh, Finn. Someone's shooting at us."

"Shooting at us? But who? And why?" Finn still shoved against him but he refused to budge, his head up listening. "Jacob?"

He shook his head. "Finn! Stop now!" He turned his head to listen. "Okay. This is what we're going to go. See how the foundation follows along to the trees. We need to crawl that way and get under better cover. We can hide there until we find the others."

"Crawl? Are you serious?" Finn stared at the face so close to hers.

"We have to, Finn. There's no other way to stay low enough." He ducked more shards of stone. "Now! Let's move." He shoved at her and she finally moved, staying as low as she could, Jacob right behind her.

Jacob finally reached for her hand and pulling her with him, ran the few feet to the trees, ducking as splinters of bark flew around them. He searched the woods, finally seeing Blackie, but not Josh or Simon. He pulled her deeper into the woods, then headed towards Blackie.

"Jacob! Finn! Thank God you're okay." Blackie had turned as he heard their quiet footsteps, ready to do battle with an attacker. "Josh is fine. He's pinned down to our right. Simon's trying to work his way around to where the shooter is."

Jacob settled Finn down behind a large fallen tree, making sure she would stay, before he turned back to Blackie.

"I don't get this, Blackie. Who knew we would be here?"

Blackie shot a look at Jacob, then shrugged. "The only one I can think of would be your lawyer. I think he's been playing you all along. It's just never felt right, the clues and what we've found." He searched the woods, finally catching sight of Simon entering the clearing from the other side. "I have asked around. No one remembers your grandfather being here in the last year. But they do remember Norman.”

“So you’re saying he did all this? Arranged all this.” Jacob sank back on his heels. “You’re right, you know. This has never felt like Grand. He wouldn’t have us running around like this.” He peered through the trees, feeling Finn’s hand on his back. “He must have left, whoever the shooter was.”

“And I don’t like that.” Simon spoke from the edge of the clearing, Josh at his side. “We need to get out of here.”

“But first, I want to show you something. I found the treasure Grand left me.” Grasping Finn’s hand, Jacob led them over towards the rock. He pointed. “There. That’s the treasure he left me.”

The three men stood and read the inscription, then nodded. “That’s the only treasure worth having, Jacob.” Blackie spoke up. “Now, let’s get back to the cabin. I could use a hot drink. I don’t know about you.”

Finn moved around the tiny kitchen, open to the rest of the cabin, as she listened to the four men discuss the events from earlier. She finally set the sandwiches and hot drinks in front of them, then pulled up a chair beside Jacob.

"So, if it wasn't your grandfather, Jacob, who was it? The lawyer?"

Jacob shrugged as he bit into his sandwich, chewing slowly as he thought through the events. Swallowing, he opened his mouth to speak, then closed it, his eyes on Blackie.

"Blackie? What're your thoughts?" Jacob turned to his friend, knowing he would be honest with him.

Blackie stared at the table, his finger pushing a crumb around as he thought. "I think your grandfather sent you here for this purpose. To remind you of your treasure in heaven. To find your past." He nodded at Finn and Jacob got his message, a slight smile on his face. "He probably said something in passing about a treasure he wanted you to find, and the lawyer decided it was money or jewels or something monetary. I think you'll find some of the letters you've been given have been written by him, not your grandfather. I called Dad earlier. He's talking to the police in your hometown. They have enough to obtain warrants and seize his computers at home and work, and any other documentation related to your grandfather and his estate."

Jacob sat back, not having expected that, but realizing that Blackie had been thinking it all through. "I think you're right, Blackie. Some of the wording just wasn't Grand. I put it off to how he was feeling."

Finn reached for his hand, hers putting pressure on his. "You never said, Jacob. How did your grandfather die?"

"They thought a heart attack. I didn't do an autopsy. I was in too much shock." He looked at her, seeing the look on her face. "You're thinking he didn't die naturally, aren't you?" He stood, running his hands through his hair, deep in thought before he turned back to the table, his hands turning white as he gripped the back of his chair. "Blackie, call your Dad. Find out how we go about doing an autopsy at this point, if it's not too late."

"Already done. He's talking to the authorities. He said he'd call you when he had the details of what needs to be done. The police were already thinking that way."

Tears gathered in Jacob's eyes. "Why didn't I see this, guys?"

Simon shook his head. "You were too close, Jacob. It was too sudden. You said your Grandfather was going to talk to you that night. That couldn't be allowed to happen, now could it?" He stood. "Let's head back to town. It's getting late. Jacob, I suggest you come back here at some point and go through what's here. I don't think you'll find anything other than what you would expect to find. Your lawyer knows he's been found out and can't get away with sending you on a wild goose chase any more."

Finn rose, reaching for the debris of their lunch, but finding Josh's hands ahead of her. He nodded towards Jacob and she turned, seeing the devastation on his face. She approached him, suddenly hugging him, drawing his attention to her. His arms came around her and he laid his head on hers. She could feel the wetness of his tears. She drew back to look up at him.

"Let's go home, Jacob. It's late."

The next morning, Finn sat in the back pew at church, the four men on either side of her, her parents, Peter and Anna in the pew in front of them. Not much had been said about the events of the day before and she was glad. That was not something she was keen to repeat.

Her attention on the bulletin she had opened, she didn't catch the look Jacob threw her and it startled her as his arm came around her and pulled her tight to him. She looked up, a frown in place, seeing the mischief in his eyes and the smile he was trying to hide.

"Jacob. We're in church." She waited for him to move his arm. It stayed in place. "Jacob? Do you think you could move your arm?" By this time, the other three men were watching them, biting back grins. "Jacob? If you hold me any tighter, I'll be on your knee. That wouldn't do at all."

Jacob took a look around, then leaned over, his breath wafting her hair from her ears as he spoke quietly. "You know, I kind of like that idea, keeping you close to me, maybe sitting on my knee. Think we can take up this conversation later?"

Finn stared at him, open mouthed, as a blush spread across her face. She could feel the pew shaking as the other three tried to control their laughter, knowing from her face that Jacob had been flirting with her.

"Jacob!" She went to continue when Timothy turned around, a frown on his face, at the slight noise.

Timothy studied his daughter flushed face, the smirk on Jacob's and the barely controlled grins on Blackie, Josh and Simon's faces before he shook his head and turned, bending over to say something to Mary, who in turn had to control her own laughter. Peter and Anna looked back, an open grin on Peter's face.

Finn turned her head into Jacob's shoulder, wishing she was anywhere else but there. Then the music caught their attention and they were immersed in the service and the sermon

Jacob listened intently, thinking it was only God who would have chosen that very scripture for that morning. Seeking Him and finding the true treasure, he thought. Grand was right. That's what he was pointing me to and reminding me of.

After the service, Finn stood talking with an older lady in church, Jacob's arm tight around her as he held her at his side. She was having trouble following the conversation with him that close, but then something the woman said caught her attention and Finn nodded, finally understanding what she was being asked.

Jacob looked around at the small church and decided he had come home. This was family, even thought he had only started attending there. He nodded and spoke to the church family, not minding the speculative glances thrown his way as they caught sight of his hold on Finn before they smiled and nodded at him.

Timothy stopped beside him, his head tilted as he studied first Jacob, then Finn, and then Jacob's hold on her.

"We need to talk, Jacob." His eyes caught Jacob's, who nodded, knowing that the conversation was already overdue.

"We do, Timothy. Do you have time this afternoon?"

"I was planning on having an afternoon-long nap and then visiting friends. I think I can work you in somewhere there." Timothy grinned at the look Jacob threw him.

"You had me going there, Timothy." Jacob grinned in return. "I'll come find you."

"You know where to find me. I'll be in the study more than likely. I have to work on the men's Bible study for Tuesday night. I'd like it if you could join us."

"I'll plan on that. Thank you."

Finn had turned just as her father walked away, a satisfied look on his face. Her brows lowered, she glanced between him and Jacob, finding Jacob watching her.

"Where to now, love?" Jacob caught her hand as they walked out of the church.

Finn stopped, her face tilted up to the fat lazy snowflakes floating down from the sky, the sound of the church carillon filling the air with Christmas hymns. She felt content and happy, a strange combination for her, she thought.

"I don't know, Jacob. We usually just spend Sundays relaxing or visiting with friends."

He nodded, drawing her with him. "Let's walk through the downtown area. I know the stores are open, but I don't shop on Sundays, not unless I have to. I'd just like to play tourist for a few hours."

"We can do that. Lunch will there when we get home, or Eddie has his hotdog cart set up in the town square."

"That sounds like a plan. I don't think I've ever eaten a hot dog in a snow storm before." He dodged the elbow she threw at him. "Let's pretend today there's no one after us. We're just friends out to spend some time together."

She studied his face once again, catching the softened look on it as he looked down at her, even as he tugged her hat lower on her hair before doing the same with his, catching her hand in his once more.

They didn't see the man who followed them all through the town, waiting for an opportunity to approach them, but not finding one. He cursed to himself. He wanted this over. Once Jacob was out of the way, he would have the Whitson fortune and own this town. That's what drove him.

Jacob turned from warming his hands over the fire and faced Timothy, who sat, open Bible on his knee, watching the younger man, remembering how it had felt when he had faced Mary's father.

"Jacob, sit. I won't bite. We've already told you how glad we are you're in Finn's life. That's not changing, is it?"

Jacob shook his head. "Not if I can help it, Timothy. She means too much to me, already. It's just this danger I'm in. I feel like I'm bringing it to her and to you."

"In a way you are, but Finn was already in danger. Thanks to you and your friends, that danger is over for her." Timothy studied the younger man. "Talk to me, Jacob. What are your feelings for my girl?"

Jacob stared at the floor, not quite sure how to respond. "I want to get to know her better, Timothy. She's precious, a treasure. One thing I do not want to do is hurt her. She's given me her trust and I don't want to break that. If it wasn't for what I'm going through."

The two men talked for a while longer before Jacob rose. He had to spend time in prayer, he knew, and today was the day he had to do that. He felt that the culmination of what he was going through was close and he needed to be prepared for that.

Chapter 17

$\mathscr{B}$lackie came looking for Jacob three days later, knowing it was going to be a tough day for him. His father had called, letting him know that he had talked to Jacob, that Aaron's body had been exhumed the day before and that the autopsy would be that day. Jacob looked up from the table in the study. Timothy had told him to start using the table there for his work, he would be family soon anyway, and had just laughed at the look Finn threw her father.

"Jacob?"

"Blackie? Aren't you working?"

He nodded. "I am. Right now, my work is to be with you. Dad called."

Jacob looked down, blinking rapidly, sorrow on his face. "I hate this, Blackie. I hate having to do this. I should have done it back then."

"Not necessarily, Jacob. Who would have thought this would have come up? I know your Grand had health issues." Blackie paused, seeing movement at the door, and watching as Finn slipped into the room and into a chair near the door. He motioned for her to come closer but she shook her head, tapping her watch. He nodded, knowing she had slipped home for a few moments, just to see how Jacob was.

"But I still should have."

"Did the authorities suggest it?"

Jacob nodded. "They gave me that option, but I just wasn't considering that it was anything but natural causes."

"Who suggested that you not do it?" Blackie waited, his eyes on Jacob, even as he heard Finn rise and come towards Jacob, pulling up a chair beside him and reaching for his hands as she sat.

"The lawyer!" He raised his head, his eyes on first Blackie and then Finn. "The lawyer told me it wasn't necessary. Now I know why. He wanted to hide what he did." His fingers gripped Finn's tightly. He paused as he heard soft words from her and realized she was praying, praying for him, for the medical examiner, for the detectives, for his friends. Then he heard her pray for the lawyer and was puzzled at that until he realized that she was right to do so. That's what we're supposed to do, isn't it, Lord, pray for those who despitefully use us? And I haven't been.

Blackie raised his head when Finn was done, watching the couple in front of him, knowing that Jacob would soon know if it was a natural death or murder.

Jacob reached and hugged Finn, listening to her speak to him before she kissed his cheek and slipped away, back to her work. He watched her go, not wanting her to, but knowing she had to. He turned back to his work, struggling to concentrate but praying that he could, that what he was creating in graphics for the churches would bring a message with them.

Hours later, he was vaguely aware of Blackie rising and leaving the room and then coming back, moving to sit beside him, just waiting for him to look up.

"Jacob? Are you at a point you can stop for the day?"

Jacob looked at him, then back at his computer screen. "Five minutes, maybe? Why?"

"We need to talk but you need to finish that first. I'll be back."

Jacob watched him walk away, then turned back, his heart sinking, knowing

Blackie likely had an answer for him and he wasn't going to like it.

He finally rose, seeing Finn standing in the doorway, and went to her, welcoming her hug.   Blackie stopped behind her, just waiting, a look on his face Jacob was familiar enough with. It would not be good news.

"Blackie?"

Blackie nodded at the question in Jacob's voice. "Let's sit. I spoke with Dad and we need to talk."

Jacob nodded, even as he dropped to the couch, Finn's hand tight in his. He looked down, not wanting to acknowledge Blackie, then sighed.

"Blackie? You have news?"

"I do, Jacob." Blackie bit his lip, not wanting to continue.

"He was murdered, wasn't he? The lawyer?"

"He was. I'm sorry, Jacob. The police will be calling you with the official report, but Dad got permission for me to tell you. The medical examiner found traces of trauma to the head. How it was missed, we don't know. The police have issued a warrant for the lawyer's arrest for murder. He's not in your hometown. They suspect he is here in Mistletoe and that he's been the one planting what you've found."

Finn finally spoke, her cheek resting against Jacob's shoulder. "That would make awful sense, now wouldn't it? How do we keep Jacob safe?"

Blackie's eyes searched first hers, then moved to Jacob, seeing his nod of comprehension. "We need to keep you safe, Finn. It's obvious to everyone you two share a bond with one another. He'll use you to get to Jacob."

"That's what I was afraid you'd say." She sighed. "I'm not giving up my life, though. I can tell you that right now."

"We don't expect you to. Dad has asked that I shadow you as much as I can. You're likely safe here at home, but at the shop, when you're out, even with Jacob, I'll be there." He looked at Jacob, making a face. "Sorry, buddy. I don't want to cut in on your budding romance."

Jacob shook his head, his eyes on Finn's head. "That's okay, I think. Is it, Finn? This is all new territory to me. I've never really dated before."

She looked up at him, a frown in place. "Is this what you and Dad talked about, what he won't tell me, just says ask you?" At his nod, she laid her head back down. "Then, yes, it's fine. Not how I ever expected to date anyone though. Stop laughing, Blackie. Your turn will come."

Blackie tried to control his chuckles but had difficulty as she frowned at him. "Sorry, guys. Finn, you're too funny for words at time."

"Stop insulting my lady, Blackie." He hugged Finn tighter. "Now what, Blackie? What does your Dad recommend we do?"

"He's going to head this way along with a couple of his operatives. They'll help by being in the background. He's trying to pull information and records but has hit a dead end on your lawyer. Norman Earl doesn't seem to exist before ten years ago."

"Norman Earl?" Finn sat up, a look of horror on her face. "No. It can't be."

"Finn? Talk to me?" Jacob reached for her hands, finding hers cold and clammy. "What about the name bothers you?"

"Blackie, tell your Dad to look for Earl Norman. It just can't be."

"What can't be?" Jacob stood and watched as Finn ran from the room, her hand to her mouth. "Blackie?"

Blackie shrugged. "I have no idea, Jacob. Let me talk to Dad." He paused, a thought crossing his mind. "Didn't you say she was assaulted when she was young and couldn't remember who it was? Did this fellow she named live here?"

"I have no idea. I'll find someone and ask." He headed for the kitchen, knowing Mary would be there. He dreaded having to bring up old news.

Chapter 18

$\mathcal{F}$inn walked slowly through the downtown area. Jacob had asked her to meet him near the Christmas tree that noon, and she had readily agreed. It had been two days since Blackie had broken the news about Jacob's grandfather and he had been really quiet. She searching, finding him watching her approach him, a large smile on his face. She walked into his hug, relishing how cherished he made her feel.

She tilted back her head to look up at him. "Jacob? You wanted a hot dog from Eddie's cart?"

He laughed as he hugged her tighter. "Not really. I just wanted to see you. We need to talk at some point about where we see us going, but today, let's find somewhere we can just sit. Your mom sent a picnic lunch if you want."

"Mom did? Wow! She's really wrapped around your finger, isn't she?"

He laughed as he reached for the pack he had set down. "No. She's just helping out a budding romance. She told me she remembers how she felt when she and your dad were dating, how the little things were more important than anything else.”

“Mom said that?” Finn turned to walk with him, her hand in his. “Is that what we are? An ‘us’? A budding romance?”

“I would like to think so. That is, if it’s okay with you.” He watched her face intently.

“It is, Jacob. You make me feel so different from anyone else. I’ve prayed about this and I know God’s hand is in it.” Her words faded away even as her steps slowed until she had stopped walking, people bumping into them, some walking around them with glares, others with words of apology.

“Finn?” Jacob looked around, not seeing anything to be concerned about. “Finn? Why did you stop?” He felt her hand tighten on his. “Finn?”

“Well, well, well. Look who we have here. Finola Bronagh. I though you had died that day.”

Jacob could feel Finn shaking in fright, but couldn’t see the speaker. The voice was familiar but he couldn’t place it. A movement to his left caught his attention and he watched in horror as a man emerged from the crowd and ripped Finn's hand from his. An arm snaked around her waist, holding her arms tight to her body, and a knife appeared, held to her throat. His eyes raised, he saw the man they had all been looking for standing in front of him, holding the love of his life literally in his hands.

"Norman? Put down the knife. Let's talk."

"There's nothing to talk about. You ruined it all. You should have just let sleeping dogs lie, or in this case, left your grandfather buried." He tightened his hold on Finn, the knife waving towards him, even as the crowd realized there was an armed man in their midst and they moved back, some almost running to get away. They kept Blackie and his father's men from getting to Jacob and Finn.

"There is always a reason to talk. I just want to know why?" Jacob moved forward slightly, determined to get to Finn.

"Your grandfather had a fortune, one you never knew about. I deserve it. I was chased from this town years ago. Partly her fault." The knife headed for Finn's face and she ducked even as she gave a small scream, startling the crowd into moving back into a tighter mass, blocking Blackie where he had managed to get closer to his two friends. "You don't deserve it."

"No, this is not about money, is it? It's about power. That's what you want. You want power and think by trying to take over this town you'll get it. You'd never get that, even if you got Grand's fortune. The town charter precludes that."

"That can be changed. We all know that." He shoved Finn forward, the knife now waving at Jacob. "You can sign over your share to me."

Jacob shook his head. "Sorry, but I can't. The charter is very clear. I've had someone look into it, someone well versed in that kind of challenge. It's iron clad. If you kill me and get control of Grand's fortune, that's all you get. The portions of town land and buildings he owns goes to the other four founding families. Even if you got rid of us all, you'd never get the town. That's been taken care of." He reached out a hand. "Come on now. Let me have the knife."

"Not happening." He turned his attention to the crowd and then back to Finn. "She'll die first. You'll watch her die before you do."

Jacob shook his head in sorrow. "That's not going to happen, Norman. Or should I call you Earl?" He saw Finn's recognition of the name. "It wasn't bad enough that you beat Finn up years ago, leaving her to die? Now, you want to finish it. That won't happen. Finn, now."

Finn allowed her body to suddenly relax, dropping away from the knife even as Jacob sprang forward. She felt herself released and then pulled away from the men, safe in Blackie's arm. He turned her from the fight, handing her off to Josh, even as he moved forward.

A groan from Jacob caught his attention and he sprang forward, taking Norman down, even as Jacob collapsed, a hand to his arm.

Blackie shoved the man at Tom who had appeared through the crowd and handcuffed him, dropping to his knees beside Jacob, hands reaching to assess him.

"Whit? Are you okay?"

Jacob nodded. "He caught my arm with the knife, but I don't think he did much damage." He looked around, his face white. "Help me sit up. I don't want Finn to see me on the ground."

"Too late for that, Whit." Blackie looked up as Finn moved into Jacob's space, tears on her face, her hand helping to remove his jacket. "Just a flesh wound. You're fortunate, Whit. I thought it was worse. I thought he got you in the stomach."

"His elbow did. That's what threw me off and let him slice me." He looked at his arm, then at Finn. "Help me up. Please. I want away from this crowd."

Blackie's hand steadied Jacob and then led him to Finn's shop, where she shoved him down in her chair and fetched the first aid box for Blackie.

She stood, watching Jacob's face. "It was really Earl Norman, Jacob?"

"It was. I wasn't sure, Finn. No one knew where he went when he left here. It's finally over for you." He watched as she struggled with the knowledge.

"And it's over for you as well, isn't it, Jacob? You have the answers you were sent here to find?"

Blackie took a look at them, then moved away, letting them have privacy. Jacob nodded to him, then reached for Finn, drawing her down on his knee. "I did, Finn. I found the treasure Grand wanted me to find.

My faith. But more than that, I found a more precious treasure than I ever dreamed of finding.”

She looked at him, her hands captured in his, not sure what he was saying. “And that is?”

“You, my love. I found you. Please don’t shove me away.”

Finn shook her head. “I couldn’t even if I wanted to. And I don’t.” Her last few words were quiet, but loud enough that Jacob caught them.

His arms drew her close as his mouth found hers, capturing her lips in their first kiss. He leaned his forehead on hers finally. “I talked to your Dad. He’s welcomed me to the family. But it’s up to you, love, where we go from here.”

Finn nodded, glad Jacob was the man of God he was. “We’ll take it slow, Jacob. You’ve been through a lot and you need to heal from that first. I’m not going anywhere.”

“Neither am I, love. Neither am I.”

Blackie approached them later at the B&B, finding them sitting on the couch in the living room, staring at the fire.

Jacob raised his head, not knowing if he would like what he had to hear.

"Jacob? Finn? You're both okay? Good." Blackie looked at his hands. "Simon will be by later, but I have news. Chief Adams has been found and charged. I'm not sure what all he's facing. Simon can tell you that. Dad had more information on Norman. He was in this town and has admitted to being the one who attacked you, Finn. He won't say why but speculation is that he was jealous even then of the ancestry you can trace back. His family was never great, into crime for years. He's facing a number of charges.

"He has admitted that he planned to take over the practice of your old lawyer, Whit. He had no relation to him, making that up. He had never been to law school, his certificates and diplomas are forged. We speculate that your grandfather had suspicions about him and was ready to pull all his legal work and take it elsewhere. Norman didn't want that. As to why he killed your grandfather, he's not saying."

"I suspect he thought if Grand was out of the way and he could get rid of me, he'd bring forth a new will, forged of course, leaving everything to him. Have them search for that, if you will." Jacob sat back, his hand held tight in both of Finn's. "It doesn't really matter now, does it?"

Blackie shook his head. "It doesn't. Your Grand sent you back here to find your roots. I think Norman took it one step further, sending you on that hunt, something I don't think your grandfather would have done."

"No, I don't think he would have. He would have left a letter directing me back here and who to talk to about the town and my ancestry and that never happened." He looked down at Finn. "But somehow, Blackie, I don't think we're done. There's still something out there that's unresolved, and I can't determine which one of us four that it involves. We're the newcomers to town. It has to be one of us or Finn would have solved the problem years ago."

"I think you're right, Whit." Blackie sat back, his eyes on the fire as well. "God kept you safe. You may have felt like you were hunting in vain, but you weren't. You found your treasure." With that, he rose and walked away, leaving Finn and Jacob together.

Epilogue

$\mathscr{S}$hedding his suit coat, Jacob moved through Finn's store six months later, his eyes searching for his love. Anna waved at him. Finn had taken Anna on as a partner, pleasing both ladies.

"She's upstairs in the apartment, Jacob. She didn't think you'd be back yet." Anna grinned as he dropped his briefcase and coat in the office and then headed for the stairs.

"I didn't expect to be either but the meetings went well and quickly. You're sure she's upstairs? She's been known to disappear a time or two."

Anna started to laugh. "I'm sure. She just headed up there with some flowers or plants or something, I think. She said she wanted it ready for us before the weekend." Peter and Anna had married about a month ago, and Finn had had the apartment upstairs remodelled for them as a thank you.

Jacob grinned as he took the stairs two at a time, searching for his lady love in the apartment. He found her in the room she had designated at the office. He leaned against the door jamb, hands in his suit pants pockets, a smile on his face as he watched her move around the room, a smile on her face, humming a worship song from the Sunday before.

Finn paused, sensing eyes on her, turning, her face lighting up as she saw Jacob standing there, running towards him. He caught her close, a kiss dropping on her lips, as he hugged her.

"You're back early!" Finn leaned back. "How come?"

"The meetings went well. I've gotten some new contracts. That new office in my house will come in handy. Thank you for designing it."

She hugged him again. "I'm so glad." She grabbed his hand. "Come look through the apartment. Tell me what you think and if I missed anything."

They wandered through, their voices quiet as they discussed it, ending up in the living room, near the large bay window. Jacob watched the afternoon light play across her face, falling further in love with her.

Finn looked around. "Have I missed anything, Jacob, that you can see? I don't think I have but it's been a crazy few months."

Jacob's eyes were on her face. "I think you've covered just about everything for them, Finn. If not, you can also add to what you've done after they move in. Peter and Anna are so happy with the apartment."

"I know. I think they'll be happy here." She turned in a circle. "But I still think I've missed something." She took a step to move away, stopping as he caught her hand. "Jacob?"

He moved in front of her. "I think you did miss one thing, love."

"I did?" She turned in a circle. "I don't see what. What did I?" She turned back to find him on his knee, a beautiful ruby ring held up in his fingers. Her hand went to her mouth as he reached for her left hand, holding it tightly.

"Just this, love. Over the last few months, I have come to love a beautiful, sensitive, caring, God-fearing, God-following woman who makes every day a joy for all around her. She cares for her family and her friends, works tirelessly to make life better for those around her who have less than she does. Finola, I love you more than I thought I could ever love anyone. That love has grown each and every day. You are a treasure that Grand didn't see coming, I don't think, even though he prayed for you every day of his life. Will you marry me, grow old with me, help me to find the treasure in life that God has for us?"

Finn nodded, unable to speak as tears flowed down her face. She finally found her voice. "I will, Jacob. I will. You are my treasure as well. I love you deeper each day. God has prepared you just for me."

He slid the ring on her finger, then stood, sweeping her into his arms and sealing their vow with a kiss. Thank you, Lord, was his thought. You have provided a lady for me to love, whose worth is far about the rubies You created.

Dear Readers

Thank you for picking up the story of Jacob and Finola, his Finn, as she's called by those who love her. Jacob had no idea when he walked into Mistletoe what God had in store for him. He certainly didn't expect to own part of the town.

He found his town, his ancestry, and more importantly, a lady to love, whose worth he decided was far about rubies. Finn found the love of her life, despite the search and trouble they both faced

My father often quoted Proverbs 31 when describing godly woman. He never said, but I suspect this is how he viewed my Mom. As I write this, his 92nd birthday is fast approaching as is the sixth anniversary of his graduation to heaven. I miss his words of wisdom and his quiet dry humour. I miss his "you did a wonderful job" when I've accomplished a renovation around the house. Dad is how I pictured Jacob's grandfather, a quiet man of few words but with a great love of family and a deep love of God.

Where is your treasure? Here on earth or up in heaven? I know where mine is. In heaven. God has given that confidence of that. He has also promised that if we seek him with all our hearts we will find Him.

Jacob was sent on a hunt for an earthly treasure, instead finding the reminder of where his greatest treasure is. My prayer for you, my readers, is that you find that great treasure God has for you.

Blessings.

Ronna